THE CARROT, THE STRING, AND THE STICK

A NOVEL

BY

DONALD SINCLAIR

authorHOUSE®

AuthorHouse™ LLC
1663 Liberty Drive
Bloomington, IN 47403
www.authorhouse.com
Phone: 1-800-839-8640

This is a work of fiction. All of the characters, names, incidents, organizations, and dialogue
in this novel are either the products of the author's imagination or are used fictitiously.

Published by AuthorHouse   04/02/2014

ISBN: 978-1-4969-0288-7 (sc)
ISBN: 978-1-4969-0289-4 (e)

Library of Congress Control Number: 2014906403

Any people depicted in stock imagery provided by Thinkstock are models,
and such images are being used for illustrative purposes only.
Certain stock imagery © Thinkstock.

This book is printed on acid-free paper.

Because of the dynamic nature of the Internet, any web addresses or links contained in
this book may have changed since publication and may no longer be valid. The views
expressed in this work are solely those of the author and do not necessarily reflect the views
of the publisher, and the publisher hereby disclaims any responsibility for them.

In medieval times, when a donkey balked at pulling an overloaded cart, the driver tied a carrot on a length of string, then, fixing it on the end of a pole, dangled the carrot out in front of the animal. The donkey pulled forward in a never-ending attempt to get the carrot.

CHAPTER 1

"Don't drink that," Marci said in her deep-rolling voice, "it's Elliott's—he knows he left it here."

"You sure?" Matt asked looking at the quarter-inch of Black and White scotch in the bottom of the pint bottle, then setting it back on the kitchen shelf. There was a snap-shot of Elliott on the shelf, wearing a cowboy hat and holding a hunting rifle.

"Yes I'm sure," she said brushing the snow off her coat hung over a kitchen chair, then reaching to take a bundle of disposable diapers out of the shopping bag sitting on the chair. "So you got to make yourself scarce—after tonight."

"Count on me," Matt said grinning. Elliott was Marci's latest attempt for a secure life. He was a wealthy architect with an office in Santa Fe, but he also had a wife and four kids down there. After Elliott divorced his wife, he and Marci were planning to move to Seattle.

"There's three Budweisers in the fridge," Marci said taking a can of baby formula out of the bag and putting it in the cabinet over the sink. "Leave one for me—I got to feed the baby now."

"Okay," Matt said closing the refrigerator door, then brushing the melting snow off his coat front as he sat down at the table. "I need a drink—bad."

He reached up for the bottle opener on a string that hung from a cartwheel chandelier overhead.

"Did you see all those bottles of booze on that shelf behind the check-out counter at the supermarket?" he said and slowly took a long drink of beer. "You could have a party for a solid week—you and your friends."

"Yeah," Marci said from the stove where she was warming the baby's food, "that's a lot of firewater." Then when she began to stir the formula with a spoon she hesitated, and asked, "What's your last name? I know your first name is Matthew—"

"Coates," he said grinning. "You know, like the coat you put on to keep warm."

"My last name is Bartlett," she said turning to look at him, smiling. "You know, like the pears."

She looked like a pear, Matt thought, in that loose tan sweater and her round rump in those cord slacks she seemed to wear most of the time. But there was more to her than looks that made her attractive; the way she talked, she let you know she would keep up her part of any love-making.

She was hard for a man to resist, and Matt found that out last night when they met in the Pueblo Bar over in the Taos Plaza. They were both drunk when they came to her house late and made love, and Matt, fell off the narrow bed in the studio room, and they both laughed out loud.

That was when Marci said, putting her hand over Matt's mouth, "Sh-h, we'll wake Margret—she's got school tomorrow."

"Margret?" Matt whispered.

"My daughter—by my first husband," she told him. "She's a teenager."

Naked in the dark, Matt was not interested in how many husbands she had, he liked instead to listen to her low voice, that some people called a "Whiskey Voice," that reeked with sex.

Her husky voice is what first attracted him at the bar, when he heard her talking with another woman at a table.

As he watched her, she took a paper matchbook, and stripping off the striking part, put it in her mouth. He figured either she was chewing the cardboard, or was eating the striking surface for the sulfur. It made him grin—she was the kind who does not care what people think.

After their fifth round of margaritas, Matt heard her say to her lady friend, "I'm going to make love to that beautiful thing sitting at the bar."

Later, when Matt walked with Marci across the highway to a short lane opposite the Taos Plaza, he saw a sign on the board fence. And when he asked her what Ufer House meant, she told him she lived in a historical studio, that Ufer was one of the artists who turned Taos into an art colony for painters.

Inside, the main room had a skylight that ran up to the high ceiling that faced north. There was a low bed in the space under the skylight, and in front of an adobe fireplace on the right, there was a couch. Back by the doorway, there was a small kitchen on one side, and on the other side a stairwell to the upstairs rooms.

Now, this morning they had been to the supermarket for baby food and diapers, and did not buy any beer or whiskey; neither of them had any money, and the baby items were on account that the state paid.

Matt was still at the table, sipping beer, when Marci came down from feeding the baby.

"Let's make love," she said putting the bottle and pot in the sink. "C'mon, before the kids come down."

When she whispered in the low voice, she was even more compelling than before.

When Matt stood up, she grabbed his crotch. They flung off clothes crossing to the bed in the studio room, and when Matt climbed up on her, holding the low bed rail, she said, "C'mon, boy—get moving."

She began to moan as he thrust hard, and then, when she climaxed, he could feel where he was inside her, everything coming down, dropping, like her insides were going to come out.

Laying side by side, their faces touching, she said to his ear, "We—should—get married."

Matt smiled, but kept his face turned away from hers.

She was rubbing the side of his arm, when she said slowly, "I need a cigarette."

"Yeah," Matt said sliding out from under the blanket, "me too."

He came back wearing his Levi's and sat on the edge of the bed, his bare feet on the floor, lighting Marci's cigarette, when he heard the outside door swing open.

Matt looked at her for a moment, recognizing her as the woman who had been at the table in the bar with Marci; she darted into the kitchen holding a bag of groceries in front of her.

Walking quickly in bare feet on the cold floor, he looked in the kitchen door just as she was taking off her jacket showing a slim and curving body.

"Did you bring any beer?" he whispered.

"I bought a six-pack," she said quietly, and after lifting a box of Cheerios and a loaf of bread out of the bag, held up six cans of Coors.

"You're a life-saver," he said looking at the slope of her breasts, the nipples showing through the jersey that was skin tight above her Levi's.

"It's not very cold, she said catching him looking, at the same time breaking out one of the silver cans from the pack.

"I'm Matt Coates," he said popping open the can, and after stopping the foam with a thumb, took a quick drink.

"I'm Karen," she said pulling open the refrigerator door, sliding the cans in, grinning. "Karen Blairmore." Then, holding her head to one side, asked "You a painter?"

"No, I'm a bum," he said sipping beer quickly. "I just got out of the army. I was in Germany almost two years. When I quit college, they drafted me into the army." Taking a double swallow of beer, "Where you from?" he asked running his tongue over his lips, as he sat down on a kitchen chair.

"Santa Monica, originally," she said filling the electric coffee pot, aware he was looking at her behind in the tight Levi's. Then as she was measuring coffee spoonfuls, with a red plastic spoon, she said slowly, "More recently from Venice-California. That's where I met Marcelline."

"Hey," Marci said coming through the doorway, "quit talking about me." She was carrying the baby in a basket and set it on the table. "Let me join the party—you two."

"Later, some time," Matt said getting to his feet, setting the empty can on the table, "Alex wants me to help swab out the bar in the mornings; he asked me yesterday."

"What's he going to pay you?" Marci asked reaching for the can of baby formula from the cabinet, her deep voice, hard, business-like.

"He pays me in beers," Matt said pulling on his shirt. "Five days in Taos," he said putting on his shoes while sitting on the bed, "and I got a job—obligations—already."

Pulling on his quilted jacket, he said, "Come to the bar—we'll party there—everybody."

When he jerked open the door, the cardboard over the broken window above the latch flapped open, letting in blowing snow, until he slammed it closed again.

CHAPTER 2

Matt crossed the highway, which was clear of snow, into the Taos Plaza, a U-shape collection of shops with porticos covering the walkways.

In the center of the Plaza, now heaped with piles of snow, was a small park with a few trees that were near the top of the town jail.

The jail was a cellar with a flat top that showed two feet above ground with bars all around. In warmer weather the heads of the prisoners could be seen. But in winter, with the blowing snow, the jail was not used.

Ahead of Matt, walking with his hand in his pockets, shoulders hunched, was the town hotel off to the left. Next to the hotel was the Pueblo Cantina, the bar where Matt worked.

The lady that owned the hotel, the tallest building in the plaza, two stories, had a son with a collection of D. H. Lawrence water colors, and for a dollar, would let tourists view the paintings.

Matt read in the biography of Lawrence he found in the town library, that he was the author of "Lady Chatterly's Lover," and lived here in Taos in the 1920s—before he headed to Mexico—and later wrote "The Plumed Serpent." Matt spent a lot of time in the library his first few days in Taos, before he made friends at the bar. He wrote eleven pages of his novel, sitting in a comfortable chair in the homey atmosphere of the small library. The working title of his book was "The Carrot, The String and The Stick."

Now, when Matt pulled open the cantina door, he saw two of the town tough-guys talking to Alex behind the bar, then he caught a glimpse of the money he was sliding to Pablo, and knew Alex had been tapped for a loan.

There were no other customers in the barroom.

"Take out the empties," Alex said to Matt over the heads of the two Mexicans. "Where you been?—It's late."

"Marci's," Matt said rounding the far end of the bar.

"Tell her," Alex said grinning, "you've got other duties—here at the bar—lover boy."

Nodding and grinning, Matt stooped down to pull the tub of empty beer cans from under the bar. It was a wide, galvanized tub with handles on each side, and though not heavy, was awkward to hold in front of you and walk.

"Last night was a good night," Matt said carrying the tub around the bar, "the tub's almost full."

"Yeah," Alex said to Matt following the two toughs to the door, "better than average."

Neither of the toughs held the door open for Matt, and he used his back to hold it open, and then swung the tub through the doorway. They must have sensed what he thought of them; it must have showed in his attitude, he could not help but think to himself as he walked in the snowy alley that ran along the bar, back to the trash can.

The bar owner, Alexander Simmons III, was a rich kid, Matt realized one afternoon when they were talking in the bar, after Matt said he was from Michigan. Alex had been stationed with a missile battery in Charlevoix, Michigan.

Alex said his family had once owned a foundry in Colorado, until copper was found. The foundry was making cast-iron stoves, but switched to smelting metals.

Alex went to Culver Military Academy and had been an officer with the anti-aircraft NIKE detachment in Charlevoix. He met Doris, his wife, up in Michigan. She had two daughters by a previous marriage, so she did not come to the bar often, spending time with the two school-aged girls at the house Alex bought south of town.

The Pueblo Cantina itself had the insides like most any other bar in America; a wood bar, a back bar with large mirrors and rows of liquor bottles, but out on the floor were low round tables and small brightly-painted chairs with wicker seats, these beneath the walls covered with hanging large sombreros and ponchos that were spread out to show their rainbow of bright colors.

Matt never asked Alex if the Cantina was named after the Indian Pueblo, a historical site, north of Taos, where the tradition of long hair braids, and wearing blankets around the body, was still done today by the native Indians who lived in the sprawling mud-brick structure in what is called today an apartment house. There was no electricity in the Pueblo someone told Matt; it is still as it was in ancient times.

"So, you and Marci mixed it up last night," Alex said to Matt sitting at the bar, after he vacuumed the floor, wiped the tables, and sat down on a stool. "You better be careful," he added when sliding a can of beer to Matt, grinning under his horn rim glasses that seemed to make his smile into a wide smirk. "I hear Elliott is in town."

"You better be careful too," Matt said reaching for the beer. "Loaning the local yokel drug dealers seed money—"

"Yeah," Alex said looking away, up the bar to the window that overlooked the plaza, "but it keeps them from breaking in here at night after hours."

Matt was drinking beer, but could see Alex go to the cash register and take out a cloth bag from behind it. "I look at it as kind of—insurance."

"I think," Matt said quietly, "you could call it 'protection money.'"

"Okay," Alex said, "call it what you want, but it works—they keep the hippies up at Arroyo Hondo in marijuana—penny-ante stuff."

Matt nodded then finished the beer in the can.

"Who is the girl Karen, from California?" Matt asked. "She's making camp at Marci's. What's her story?"

Alex smiled and shook his head, and looking at Matt said, "Marci brought her out here to live with Kozlo, the painter. He came here from Poland—and I hear he sells a lot of paintings in Santa Fe—and even in California."

"She's a little on the thin side," Matt said, but she sticks out in all the right places—and when she looks at you—you can't help get excited. She's sex on roller skates—she don't have to say anything—"

"Stay away from her, Matt," Alex said taking money from under the cash tray in the register, last night's receipts. "You'll really mess her up if Kozlo finds out—she'll be back on the street," he said zipping up the bag. "I'm going to the bank. Serve any customer that shows up—I'll only be a few minutes."

"All right," Matt said and, after Alex went out, walked behind the bar, then threw the empty can into the tub, making a loud, tinny pang. "What the hell," Matt said, then took another beer, grinning, saying, "he expects me to take another—he seems to know everything around town."

When Alex came back into the bar he was followed by a rumpled man who, Matt thought, looked like one of those giant sheep dogs.

"This is Monk," Alex said to Matt, who was walking around the end of the bar. "He was the day bartender for the previous owner—the one I bought the bar from."

Matt shook hands, looking at the full-face beard, a baggy cable-knit wool sweater, baggy wool pants, and hair that was curly in all directions.

"Alex says you're a writer too," Monk said. "I write poetry. I got a lot of lines done until my tooth infected—I came to town to get it fixed—I'm holed-up in an abandoned adobe in the hills above the Indian Pueblo."

"Is that why they call you Monk?" Matt asked, "because you live in the hills."

"No, no," Monk said grinning. "My last name is Merton, the same as Thomas Merton who wrote "The Seven Story Mountain" book—the guy who later became a Trappist monk and is living in a monastery somewhere in Kentucky."

"What's your first name?" Matt asked.

"Wesley, but just call me Monk—like everybody does."

The telephone rang, and Alex scurried around the bar to answer it up at the end near the window.

Matt tipped up the beer can he was holding, finishing what was in the bottom.

"Well," he said, "I'm done cleaning up here for today, so I'm leaving." He reached over the bar and dropped the can in the tub.

"I can't drink," Monk said sitting down on a barstool. "The dentist gave me a ton of antibiotics."

"O-oh," Alex said talking on the phone. Then he rested his elbow on the bar and put his hand on his forehead. "Okay, okay," he said looking down at the floor.

Setting the phone on the cradle slowly, Alex said, "My wife's sister just passed away up in Michigan."

"Was it all of a sudden?" Monk asked.

"No, she's been sinking for almost a year," Alex said and took two bottles of Hamm's beer out of the top cooler. "She had Lymphoma," he said setting the two bottles on the bar; beer that was sold to tourist customers. "I'm going to have to ask you guys for help."

"Sure, anything," Matt said taking one of the bottles.

"Doris wants to take our car up—drive to Michigan—she'll need the car up there to get around with the girls," Alex said. "She's too upset to drive all that way—I'm going too—to do the driving."

"How can we help?" Monk asked.

"I'll be gone about a week—or so—and I want you to run the bar for me while I'm up there."

Matt swallowed his beer quickly, and holding the bottle out from his face said, "I don't know how to run a bar." He leaned back on the stool. "I only know about the customer side of the bar."

"I'll help you," Monk said. "I'll show you the ropes." He reached for the beer on the bar and took a quick drink.

CHAPTER 3

Wen Elliott did not show up at Marci's the next morning, and Matt heard about it at the bar from Alex, Matt went shopping with the money he set aside for the rent.

It was 8:15 when he finished his cleaning work at the bar, and then did the shopping at the supermarket.

At the front door of Marci's studio house, he had to juggle the bag of groceries to slide his hand under the piece of cardboard in the window to unlock the bolt.

Marci and Karen were painting a canvas with white paint. The canvas was so large it nearly covered the wall.

"Look who showed up," Marci said turning to look at Matt, the paintbrush in her hand dripping white paint. "Don't you have a home?"

"I like it here better," he said watching both women smile.

He saw that both were only wearing t-shirts, Karen's breasts coming to a curving point, Marci's hanging flat.

"I see you've been shopping," Marci said as she made up and down strokes with the brush just above her head, the canvas quivering.

"I bought eggs," Matt said looking in the bag. "They're my stock in trade—since Alex gave me the hard boiled egg concession for the bar."

"How much do you make?" Marci asked without turning, dipping her brush in the paint can.

"Three bucks," Matt said, "on my investment of thirty-nine cents."

"Only," Karen said smiling, "if you sell them <u>all</u> in one day," and bent to dip her brush in the can next to Marci.

"Yeah," Matt said, "sometimes it takes four-five days to sell them all."

He saw both women look at one another.

"Maybe I can boil my eggs in the kitchen," he said to Marci.

"Go ahead," she said. Then asked without turning, "that all you got in the bag?"

"No," he said watching Marci stretch to paint the upper right corner of the canvas, "I got day-old raisin bread and a jar of peanut butter—and a pack of bologna. And a six-pack of Coors."

"Boiling eggs will cost you," Marci said looking at Karen and grinning. "My fee is a can of Coors."

"I figured," Matt said walking back to the kitchen door, then stopped. "You want a beer Karen?"

"Not now," she said, and he caught her looking at him, in that way of hers, that was saying she was available and miserable at the same time.

Marci was different; she knew how to get the best out of the moment. Like the time she wanted to make love before the kids came down to breakfast, the other day. She knew how to make things—urgent—almost frantic—by shortening the time span, so the lovemaking would be more frantic, intense.

"I'm going to put my groceries in the frig until I go," he said. He knew that Elliott was not coming today, and now he told Marci he knew. Then before stepping into the kitchen, he asked, "What—you going to paint on the king-size canvas—the Grand Canyon—or something?"

"We're prepping it for Sunday," Marci said turning to look at him. "We're going to have a painting party—everybody that comes has to paint a square given to them."

"I can't paint," Matt said. "I'm a writer," he said swinging his free hand. "I don't know how to paint."

Karen was painting over the part of the giant canvas where lily-pads had been painted on a small pond. It was the beginning of a painting on the large canvas that some had started and never completed.

She turned suddenly, smiling, and caught Matt looking at her round bottom as she stooped to paint.

"You'll think of—something—to paint," she said to him. "Just think of something you like—or want—and make a picture—painting—of it."

Shifting his view to the back of Marci, Matt saw a wider bottom in the cord slacks, but well rounded.

"Can't you leave the lily-pads alone?" Matt asked. "I think they're relaxing—tranquil—restful."

Marci dipped her brush into the can of paint, and with paint dripping to the floor, made wide stokes, covering the lily-pads in front of Karen.

"I could use that beer," Marci said, but was really saying "'Too late now—the lily-pads are gone.'"

Matt saw Karen smiling over the give-and-take between him and Marci. She was enjoying the banter, dipping her paintbrush into the can; she began moving her hips from side to side. She knew his eyes were on her.

She knew too, they had made love; she saw him on the floor that morning Matt spent the night with Marci; she was interested in him and was telling him so with her movements.

He liked knowing she was willing; he smiled, then turning, pulled himself through the kitchen doorway.

Taking a large aluminum pot from under the sink, he began filling it with water from the spigot, when Marci came through the doorway, wiping her hands on a rag that was a piece of a t-shirt.

"Don't use aluminum," she said walking up behind him. "You're supposed to use steel—or a porcelain pot."

"How come?" Matt said turning to her.

"I don't know for sure," she said, "but, aluminum does something to the eggs—makes them taste funny."

"Okay, okay."

"There's more pots there under the sink."

Matt, shaking his head at Marci's assurance and confidence in herself, bent down and found a gray speckled pot.

Smiling, he emptied one pot into the other and set it on the burner.

"Anything else?" Matt said sarcastically, but not meaning it, being playful with her.

"Use a medium flame," she said quietly in her rolling voice. "And find a lid."

"Okay, okay," he said.

She was watching him putting the eggs in the water, when she said quietly, "I'm glad you came by now, Matt." Then reaching up with her hand on his neck, kissed him. "I need you."

"I came by," he said, "hoping we could—be together again—spend some time—alone."

"We will," she said. "Just wait a bit—in a little while. Be patient, honey."

He felt her hand on his scrotum, cupped and holding.

"Damn," he whispered, "there's more than eggs boiling," and putting his arm around her, added, "let's do it right here."

"Hold on, my sweet," she said when he was holding the length of her against him. "I want it too, but just wait a bit. Plea-ase."

When he kissed her again, he pulled her rump up, almost lifting her.

"No, no," she said pushing him, "it's not the right time, honey."

"Karen don't care," he said.

"It's not Karen," she whispered looking up. "Elliott may show up any—time. We—I have to be careful."

"This you and Elliott thing," he said, "is harder on me—than it is for you two."

"I know, honey," she said putting her arms around his waist, "but let me find out—what Elliott is going to do—for sure—finally—about leaving Santa Fe. If he's going to move in up here—or not."

"I don't see what difference it—" Matt began.

"Don't say it, honey," she said. "Don't put it into words. Okay," she said letting go of him.

"But my <u>time</u> is limited," Matt said. "I'm going to be tied up for a week managing the bar—maybe even longer—and not only that, I have to stay out at Alex's house," he said, "to feed the damn cat."

He turned away from her to look at the boiling eggs, lifting the pot lid.

"How do you get out to the house and back?" Marci asked smiling, amused at Matt's accepting all the new responsibility.

"I got use of Doris's Chevy," he said turning back to her after putting the lid back on the pot. "I can use it to run errands for the bar."

"Good," Marci said quietly, reaching to turn off the heat on the eggs, "you can run some errand over here too—you can come here after you close the bar."

"What if Elliott shows up?"

"We'll work around it, honey. We'll work something out."

"What can we do, if he moves in here?"

She took hold of his arms above the wrists.

"Honey, you're the writer," she said looking up at him. "You make up plots for your stories. Well, make up one—so we can be together."

"I don't—"he started.

"I don't want to lose you, honey," she said putting her arms around him. "We're good together."

She leaned against him.

"That's putting it mildly," he said to her forehead.

"You can come over from the bar—at night when it closes at two—you'll have the car—if I can get out," she said to his chest.

"No, no" he said. "I got a better idea. You come to the bar—<u>work</u> at the bar. You can help by serving the tables for me and Monk."

"That's it, honey," she said looking up. "You're a genius."

He was kissing her when Karen came to the kitchen door.

"I finished painting the canvas," she said. "The whole thing has a white coat now."

Marci turned away from Matt, and running her hand over her hair, asked, "How's the baby doing?"

"She's still sleeping," Karen said, then added, "I've got to run now—I've got shopping to do."

Matt began taking the eggs out of the pot setting them on a wire rack, using a large wood spoon.

"You deserve a beer," Matt said to Karen. "You want a Coors, Karen?"

Marci pulled open the refrigerator door and took two cans from the six-pack on the bottom shelf, handing one to Matt, after opening it. She stood with the second can, opening the top, but did not offer it to Karen.

Matt smiled; Marci did not want Karen to be around him. She was possessive of Matt, and considered Karen a competitor. It was obvious, Matt realized, they were friends, but Marci had limits on the friendship.

"No time," Karen said looking at her hands, one side, then the other, "I got to get to the pharmacy at the drug store—to pick up a prescription being filled. Kozlo has an ear infection—he takes antibiotics."

She began tucking her dark blue t-shirt into her Levi's pulling the cloth tight over her breasts, making the large nipples show.

Marci did not see her turn, giving Matt a side view, but Karen knew he was watching over Marci's shoulder and stood up erect.

"We can put the eggs in cold water," Marci said. "That will cool them faster."

She took a sip from the beer can, set it on the sink, then lifted the entire rack of eggs and set them in the sink, and turned the stopper closed, then opened the cold water tap.

"You can break eggs easily," Marci said watching the water running. "Almost by looking at them."

Matt smiled, and took another sip of beer, but did not say anything.

He stood wondering if she was jealous, or if she was just being possessive.

"Everybody knows that," he said, grinning.

"Be careful," she said in her rolling, low tone. "If Kozlo finds out—she'll be back out on the street." Then, turning off the water, she picked up her beer can. "Unless—you're planning on taking her in—and paying all the bills—hey, my sweet."

"I came here this morning," Matt said in an even voice, almost whispering, "so we could be together—like the other night. Can't we—just have that—again?"

Before Marci could answer, a shout came from the studio through the doorway.

"Hey, who's Chevy is that outside?"

Marci's oldest daughter, Elizabeth, came through the doorway; when she saw Matt, she stopped quickly, and turned to reach for a bowl in the cabinet over the stove.

"I thought you said Elliott was coming," she said to her mother, filling the bowl with cereal, while sitting down at the table.

"He'll be here in a while," Marci said, taking a carton of milk from the fridge and setting it in front of Elizabeth.

Matt was studying Elizabeth's light-blue sweater.

"I'm driving the Chevy," Matt said and set his beer can on the edge of the table. "I'm running the bar while the Simmons go up north to a funeral. I got the car to do bar errands—it's Doris Simmons' car."

"Laura Simmons is in my biology class at school," Elizabeth said, then put a spoonful of cereal in her mouth.

Marci put a towel on the sink.

"I'm going to dry the eggs," she said taking them one at a time from the sink.

"Put them right in the carton," Matt said. "Why bother drying them?"

"I'm taking driving lessons at school," Elizabeth said looking at Matt, her head to one side, making her long hair slide over the side of her face. "But I don't get any driving time—outside of school. Mom sold her car."

"Finish your breakfast," Marci said to her, "you're going to be late for school, baby."

"You're right, mom," Elizabeth said getting up from the table, pulling her sweater down tight, looking at Matt. "We got assembly this morning—I don't want to be late."

"Check Nancy in the basket," Marci said as Elizabeth was going through the doorway. Then turning to stand next to Matt, bumping his shoulder with her hip, she said, "After you close the bar—come by. Okay?"

She set the carton of eggs on the table in front of him.

"Nancy's still sleeping," Elizabeth shouted from out in the studio.

"What if Elliott's here?" Matt said.

"Then we'll both know, won't we?" Marci said.

Matt stood up and took his bologna and cheese from the refrigerator and put them in the shopping bag, then the eggs.

"Yeah, I guess we will," he said picking up the bag.

CHAPTER 4

"We're fifteen bucks short," Monk said over the bar when Matt came in the door. They had been running the bar five days.

"Not too bad," Matt said and set a carton of eggs on the bar. He had cooked them out at the Simmons' house where he stayed the past two nights.

"Yeah," Monk said and turned to pick up the canvas cash bag, zipping it closed. "It's the second time," he said pulling at his stringy beard next to his mouth, "and I—don't think it's a—coincidence."

"I didn't take it," Matt said full aware of what he was getting at.

"Yep," Monk said, "she's got sticky fingers—again."

"If I ask her for the fifteen," Matt said, "she'll hate my guts."

"You just don't want to lose Marci as a bed-partner," Monk said, "quit the bologna." Handing the money bag to Matt while shaking his head, he said, "We'll just have to keep her from handling cash."

"How can we do that?" Matt said squeezing the lump of money in the bag from last night's bar sales. "I mean, if she's going to work here?"

"We should fire her—and—" Monk began.

"We need a waitress for the tables—when things get busy," Matt said. "And she's good with the customer chatter—especially the women—"

"Okay, okay," Monk said, nodding. "She stays—if you get the fifteen back—she probably stole twice as much."

"I'll ask her for the money," Matt said quietly, then reaching for the egg carton slid it to Monk. "Put these in the bowl for me."

Behind the bar on a shelf was the bowl with a sign: HARD BOILED EGGS—TWO BITS EACH.

"You're really going to ask Marci?" Monk asked, opening the egg carton, grinning. "You're going to confront her?"

"How else can I get the fifteen back?" Matt said stuffing the cash bag in the pocket of his quilted ski jacket.

Monk smiled, disbelieving Matt about facing her for the money. Putting eggs in the bowl he said, "Hurry back from the bank, the Budweiser delivery truck comes today."

Every time he took the cash deposits to the bank, Matt felt a twinge of pride. The trust Alex had in him seemed to bolster Matt's incentive not to let him down. Alex told Matt the deposits would allow the family to write checks and cover the expense of traveling to Michigan.

At the door, Matt stopped. "Hey look," he said over to Monk, "snow is really coming down. Look out there."

"The roads are going to get slick," Monk said, bending over the bar sink, washing glasses. "Business is going to be slow today—probably."

An orange cat trotted past the door, and Matt saw it turn into the alley next to the doorway.

"Ah-h damn," Matt said pulling on his gloves, "I forgot to feed Hitler this morning. I was in such a hurry—I didn't remember."

Monk looked up, making a sour face, said slowly, "You forgot to feed the damn cat?"

The Simmons' cat was named "Hitler" by Jenny, the youngest daughter, since the cat, essentially white with rust and black blotches spread over the body, had one black blotch under its nose, making it look like the mustache Adolph Hitler wore.

"I'll go out to the house quick and feed the cat, "Matt said, "before the snow makes the roads too bad."

"Just make the bank deposit first," Monk said, his head down as he washed glasses in the sink under the bar.

Driving slow out of the parking lot behind the bar, following the telephone pole laying on its side, now with a cap of snow, he had to smile. He had seen Indians from the Pueblo, sitting on the pole, drinking from pints and talking, all wearing cotton blankets from the JC Penny department store wrapped around their heads and shoulders. Alex said the town council was going to ask the Pueblo chiefs to put a stop to the drinking because it was bad for the tourists to see.

Matt had to drive slow on the highway, with the car lights on, the wet, heavy flakes collecting on the windshield, so he could only see out where the wipers pushed away the packed snow.

Turning into the driveway at the Simmons' house, he drove slowly up to the house where he thought the driveway should be. Everything out here in the open country was already covered by the snowfall.

When he unlocked the door and opened it, the cat ran out between his feet, then stopped once outside in the whiteness, looking at the snow, then at Matt.

"Bet you're starving," Matt said holding the door open so the cat could come in. "Come on—we'll find something to eat."

The house was built in adobe style, logs across the ceiling, a fireplace the shape of a hornet's nest made of mud, but the kitchen was all modern.

Matt took a can of cat food from the cabinet, and was cutting the top off with an opener, when the cat, down on the floor, made a loud "<u>me-o-ow</u>."

"Okay, okay, Adolph," Matt said turning the can opener until the lid fell away. Then as he set the can on the floor, the cat made a leap, and landing over the food, began eating in a thrusting motion with the whole body.

On the kitchen table, Matt saw the scattered sheets of yellow legal paper that were part of his book he wrote last night. He gathered the numbered sheets, put them in sequence, then slid them into a bulging manila folder with the other pages.

Putting the large rubber band around the folder, he said, "That's nine more pages, and—that makes seventy-three total. Not bad."

The cat came over, looking up.

"You keep an eye on the house," Matt said, "I got to get back to the bar. I'll be back—late—when we close up," and for some reason he could not call the cat Hitler. "They could have named you Charlie—you look like Charlie Chaplin."

Outside, Matt backed slowly down the driveway snow, stopping the car at the mailbox. Sorting through the letters, and not finding anything addressed to him, he put them in the paper bag on the back seat with all the other mail he collected in the past days.

He drove slowly back to the highway, then joined the line of cars moving toward Taos, their headlights on, in the blowing snow.

When he saw the town signs, then the buildings, Matt turned off the highway at the Post Office, after he spotted the stars and stripes flag straight out from the pole in the flying snow.

It was then he spotted Karen coming out the lobby door. She was wearing a short jacket and high-heeled boots.

Matt felt a shock of excitement, and smiling, and peering through the opening on the windshield made by the wiper, said "She's dressed for California."

Slowing the car as he came next to her walking, her arms folded over her chest, he rolled down the car window.

"Karen. Hey Karen, jump in. I'll buzz you home," he shouted, keeping his eyes on the road.

"Oh-h," she said bending to look into the car. "It's you—Matt."

She did not hesitate; pulling open the car door and almost leaping into the seat, bringing her legs in last.

"What you doing in the Post Office?" Matt asked driving the car slowly away from the curb. "I mean—out in this snow storm?"

"I just came from the hospital," she said taking a pack of Salem cigarettes from her purse. She took one cigarette out and put it in her mouth slowly. "I've been at the hospital," she said lighting the cigarette with a paper match. "Gregory—Kozlo is in the hospital—his doctor made him go in this morning."

"No kidding," Matt said turning to the street that led to the bar parking lot. "Is it anything—serious?"

"He's got a really bad ear infection," she said blowing smoke, looking forward through the windshield where the wiper was working. "His right ear—the hearing is gone—they are going to operate."

"Wow," Matt said looking at her for a second, her tight slacks over her thighs, "that's a tough break."

"They got him on penicillin," she said in a low voice, "around the clock—intravenous—trying to stop the infection, but they want to operate, make a way for the ear to drain the infection out."

"Is it painful?" Matt asked.

"No," she said throwing her cigarette out the window, then rolling it back up. "I wanted to stay. But the doctor told me to go home—the hospital is going to call me when I can come back."

"Is all this going to effect his painting, you think?"

"No," she said, turning to Matt, smiling, "he'll go on painting angels floating over some village—in Poland—or someplace like it." She smiled saying, "His hero is Chagall."

Then, when Matt turned into the parking lot behind the bar, she looked at him, her mouth open, "Hey, where you going?"

"Back to the bar," he said looking at her a little startled by the question.

"I can't go in there," she said taking out another cigarette. "Someone will tell Kozlo I was in the bar drinking while he was in the hospital." The cigarette was in the corner of her mouth, and she twisted her face to the flame to light it.

"Yeah," Matt said, "I guess you're right," stopping the car.

"Isn't there some other place—we could have a drink?" she asked, putting her hands on her thighs and slowly pushing forward. "I need a drink—the way this day is going—where could we go?"

"I know a place," Matt said looking at the side of her face. "Back where I just came from; the Simmons' house."

"Okay," Karen said in a relieved way, "let's go there."

Matt smiled, when she straightened her legs forward, holding them together, while he turned the car around in the parking lot.

At the house, the cat stood on the kitchen counter and watched Matt mix two rum and cokes in tall glasses with pictures of running horses on the sides.

"There's no limes," he said handing Karen a glass. They both took a long drink.

"That's better," she said looking at the glass in her hand, then setting it down. "So this is where the Simmons live," she said. "Nice and—homey."

She took off her short jacket and dropped it over the back of a kitchen chair, and Matt saw she was not wearing anything under the white turtleneck sweater.

He was going to kiss her, but she picked up her drink and walked out into the front room. He followed her, and when she sat down on the couch in front of the dark fireplace, he sat down next to her.

"I'll start a fire," he said setting his glass on the low table in front of him.

"Let's skip the high school stuff," she said setting her glass on the table next to his.

She pulled up her sweater, using both hands, lifting it quickly over her head; she looked at him, her head to one side.

"Let's go to the bedroom," he said unable to take his eyes off her large nipples at the end of her full breasts.

The cat looked up at Matt, watching him close the bedroom door that left him outside.

"Hurry," Karen said sitting down, taking off her boot, and sitting on the edge of the bed.

She took down her tight slacks and undergarment at the same time. "I'm burning up," she said in a whisper.

Matt realized she was saying in affect she had enough of Kozlo.

Then, when they were making love, he heard her mutter the word "Morrow," as she thrusted back at his plunges, and he understood; she was saying, "To-morrow."

But later he said nothing, as they lie side by side, his face against her hair.

A muted phone rang out in the living room.

"Damn," Matt said turning his head to look at the door.

"Who's that?" Karen said, making a sour face, watching as Matt pulled on his Levi's. "Don't answer it," she said brushing hair sticking to her face. "Come back—so we can do it again—"

"It's probably Monk," Matt said going to the door in his bare feet. "It might be something important."

"Yeah, Matt," Monk said "thought you were coming right back from feeding the cat."

"The snow's making the roads—slippery," Matt said looking at his bare feet. "I'm waiting a bit to see if—the snow might let up—a little."

"You alone out there?" Monk asked in a kidding tone.

"No, the cat Hitler is here."

"Matt," Monk said in a fatherly tone, "someone saw Karen get in your car—over by the Post Office."

"Is that why you called?" Matt said feeling like he had been hit in the stomach. "When Kozlo gets wind of your—"

"I just gave her a ride home," Matt said in a low tone. "People can make any story they want—out of it."

"Good luck," Monk said, "on sticking to <u>that</u> story. You don't have to convince me. It's Kozlo—you got to convince."

"Okay, okay," Matt said, "now I know. Is that why you called?" he said again, and saw Karen, wrapped in a blanket, come into the living room and pick up one of the rum drinks off the low table.

"No," Monk said, "tonight we'll have the usual Saturday night crowd—and I can't handle on my lonesome. I just want to know if—when rather—you're going to show."

"An hour," Matt said watching Karen sipping the rum and coke. "Two at most," he added.

"Well, Matt, get here as soon as you can."

"You bet," Matt said and hung up the phone.

When Matt reached over and pulled the blanket, Karen let it fall to the floor, taking another sip of rum and coke.

She stood drinking for a moment, then stopped and smiled at him, knowing how her nakedness was affecting him.

Matt was going to say she had a perfect shape with all the right curves, but instead blurted out, "Does Kozlo ask you to pose—for any of his paintings?"

He knew everyone who saw her curves, said something about them—and he knew she had heard it all.

He had never met a beautiful woman who did not know she was a stand out.

"Kozlo is a frog," she said setting her glass down on the low table. "He is a stomach—with skinny arms and legs coming out."

Matt was smiling when he said, "I got to get back to the bar—"

"That don't give us much time," Karen said and reached to undo Matt's Levi's. "I like looking at you," she said pushing the pants so they dropped, "the same way you like looking at me. You know—when the opportunity—"

He kissed her, then picked her up and carried her back into the bedroom, grinning.

Later, after they showered, Matt went out to the living room to get his Levi's and left the bedroom door open. The cat followed, when Matt stepped back into the bedroom, continuing his dressing, and jumped up on the bed next to Karen as she was pulling on her boots.

"You hungry?" Matt said to Karen as he lifted his sweater over his head. "They left a lot of stuff in the fridge."

"No," she said running her hand over the back of the cat, "I'm not in the mood for eating anything."

"Okay," Matt said slipping his ski jacket on, "then I'll drive you back to the Post Office—you can pick up where you left off—from there."

"I got a better idea," Karen said slowly getting to her feet, running her hand between the ears of the cat, "you drive us to the bar—park out back and go in—then when I know you're inside—I'll get out of the car and head home."

"I don't see why—" Matt started to say.

"I got a—feeling—Kozlo is around—someplace," Karen said holding the cat's head, rubbing the fur. "Isn't that odd."

"You mean," Matt said, "he's out of the hospital?"

"Uh-huh," Karen said. "Why is the cat called Hitler?"

"The mustache—under his nose."

"Mustache?" she said lifting the cat's face. "Oh, yes, I see it now." Petting the cat, she said, "I don't know if that's funny—or not."

CHAPTER 5

Matt was hunched forward, looking through the opening of the car windshield made by the wiper in the heavy snow that covered the entire car.

All the cars had their lights on in the blizzard, and he was following the red taillights of the car ahead, keeping the ruts that was the highway now.

"You ever been married?" Karen asked as she was lighting a cigarette, her face showing in the flash for an instant.

"Almost," he said without looking at her.

"Either you were, or you weren't," she said blowing out smoke.

"I was—involved—with a girl at the university once, but when it came down to getting married, I had to tell her I wanted to see London, Paris and Rome—and Africa—and maybe China. Well, you get the picture."

"You wanted to travel, huh?"

"Yep," Matt said nodding slowly, "that and writing about it—making a living that way. Living it up—to write it down." He looked at Karen for a moment, "To answer your question, no, because I don't think I could just sit in the backyard—with the kids."

"You belong with that bunch of hippies out at the Aroyyo Hondo," Karen said blowing out cigarette smoke. "They don't think too much about—conventional life—or even sleeping in a conventional bed."

"The hippies dropped-out of the double standard life we have in America—that's all— they know everybody cheats."

Matt remembered a group of hippies he saw in California near San Francisco, when he was traveling out there, in some small town near Lodi. The hippies travelled to town in a Volkswagen van, and they walked in a group to do the shopping, he remembered; all of them wearing second hand clothes; the women and kids barefoot, hair grown long, and the men thin, like scarecrows. Some of the women were pregnant, and their faces showed a strain look.

"Okay," Karen said, "so you're not the hippy type."

"I'm more concerned with seeing places and people," Matt said, "than protesting."

"But," Karen said, "you still don't want to settle-down, you want to skip that part." She smiled. "Isn't that protesting?"

"I look at it as a vocational requirement," he said as the Taos City Limits sign appeared at the roadside through the blowing snow. "I mean—I like to keep on the go—but I still like fine foods—and clean beds."

"Matt wants it all," Karen said.

"I just know what I want," he said getting tired of bantering words.

"That's why you left the university," Karen said in a sharp tone—meant to criticize. "To come to Taos."

"No; I came from Europe—Spain mostly," he said, thinking she was beginning to sound like a wife. "I hid out in the Balearic Islands—first Ibiza, then Formentera Island."

"The way you're talking, Matt—it sounds delusional."

"People need an illusion," he said grinning. "Something that keeps them moving—a carrot out in front of them, hanging on a string—otherwise they'll keep sitting in the backyard."

"It's different for a girl," Karen said squinting at Matt in the dark, "she has to find a man that will provide the—essentials—to raise a family."

"I know," Matt said, "to start a family—you need a house, then furniture and a refrigerator, and a lawn—then a lawn mower."

"You're just dodging the facts of life, Matt," she said in the tone of a schoolteacher.

"Yeah," he said, "it's just that I want to do some things before I settle down."

"Girls have a different role," Karen said lighting another cigarette, "one that fits what they have to do in life."

"And me," he said, "I'm doing what I have to do."

"And that's what you're doing now, right?"

"Yeah," Matt said. "Exactly." He grinned, but did not look at her. "At a party once," he said slowly, "I heard two girls talking about me. One of them said, 'He's a nice guy—but he's a bum.'"

"What did you expect?" Karen said in flat voice.

Pulling into the snow covered parking lot behind the bar, he drove to the back wall and stopped.

"Well, maybe I'll find a girl that likes living out of a suitcase," he said, opening the car door.

"That would only work for a while," Karen said ducking her head level with the dashboard of the car when the dome light went on. "Go quick—I don't want to be seen."

"All right," Matt said stepping out into the snow, slamming the door quickly, not looking back, and hunching his shoulders against the blowing snow in the alley as he walked. "She's one to criticize my life," he muttered. "Look at the way she lives."

Inside the bar, Matt was surprised to see the room so crowded; the barstools all taken, and over by the juke box, three women had two tables pushed together, occupying the rear of the room.

When Monk saw Matt come in the door, he stood up from leaning on the bar, where he had been talking to a man with long hair, wearing a western jacket with fringes hanging under the arms and across the back.

Matt moved quickly behind the row of customers sitting on the stools, pulling off his wet jacket, when Monk came through the end of the bar opening and stood in front of him.

"You know who that is—in the fringe jacket?" Monk whispered.

Matt, expecting a wisecrack for being with a girl on bar work time, just shrugged. Then holding his wet jacket by the collar, he looked in the mirror behind the bar, and saw the man had a bottle of expensive Mexican beer, and he was wearing a string of what looked like bear claws around his neck.

"He looks sort of familiar," Matt said shaking the wet snow off his jacket.

"He-e's an actor," Monk said almost in a hiss. "He's Hopper. Dennis Hopper."

"Oh, yeah," Matt said. "I recognize him now."

"Is that all—" Monk said, "you got to say, for Pete's sake? We got a celebrity here in the bar tonight."

"No," Matt said smiling, "I want to say, I want to hang my wet jacket in the storeroom."

"Don't you prose writers ever get excited?" Monk said to blunt Matt's humor. "I guess not." When Matt turned to go to the storeroom, Monk said in a loud voice, "Hurry up. We got a busy Saturday night crowd."

Matt asked, walking, "Is Marci working tonight?"

"On the phone," Monk said, "she said she was waiting for Elliott to show up—she was sure he'd come up."

"The roads are all clogged up with snow," Matt said. "But you never know," he added moving down the hallway.

"Did you ask her for the fifteen bucks she took from the bar receipts?"

"I haven't been able to get her—alone," Matt said standing in the doorway to the storeroom. "I want to—ask her—when nobody can hear me ask."

Someone out at the bar called for the bartender, and Monk stepped quickly behind the bar out front.

When Matt snapped on the light, he saw the storeroom floor covered with sawdust, pieces of two-by-fours, and scraps of plywood, the carpenter had left. Alex was paneling the storeroom to make a pool hall backroom to bring in more business, and the workman was nearly done.

As Matt walked out behind the bar, he saw the throwaway tub for empties nearly full; he realized how busy Monk had been today while he was out at the Simmons' house.

Alex knew what he was doing by letting Monk run the bar, Matt thought, and then wondered if Monk was as good a poet as he was a bartender.

When Hopper called for another beer, Matt took a bottle of Dos Equis out of the cooler and set it in front of him.

"Refill this too," Hopper said holding up a shot glass.

"What is it?"

"Tequila."

Pouring tequila, Matt said, "You come to Taos for the ski-ing? I hear it's pretty good up at that Eagle Wind Resort—up north of town."

"No," Hopper said pouring beer into his glass, "I'm sight-seeing. That old Pueblo is a gas—those Indians are still living the same as their ancestors did centuries ago."

"I took a lot of pictures," he said and held up a camera by the strap. He had a carrying case of camera equipment on the floor that Matt could not see. "We were thinking of using Taos—in a movie we're planning. I'm scouting locations, taking a lot of pictures. There's a junkyard—north of town."

"You want to make a movie in Taos?" Matt asked.

"Part of the movie—maybe," Hopper said and sipped some of the beer. "I'm going up to Trinidad tomorrow—if the roads are open. But I think I'll come back here to Taos. Maybe, after the movie, settle here. Buy some land."

"What's the title of your movie?" Matt asked watching Hopper drinking his beer.

"'Valiant Riders,'" he said, putting his beer glass down on the bar. "Or maybe 'Silent Riders,' maybe—I'm still writing the script." Lighting a cigarette, he shrugged.

Matt smiled, "You going to <u>act</u> in it too?"

"Yes; me and Peter Fonda. We're the producers too."

"What kind of a story is it?" Matt asked. I write stories—what kind of a story you using for the movie?"

Before he could answer, the man sitting next to him ordered a Seven and Seven refill, and when Matt poured the Seagram's into the glass, he saw the Seven-Up bottle was empty, and went to the storeroom for another.

When Matt came back, Hopper was gone from the bar. He shook his head, disappointed because he was working up to ask Hopper if he could help with the writing of the movie scenario. Get a job.

He wanted to tell Hopper about the hippies living up on the Arroyo Hondo, that would be good for the script. But that chance was gone now, and he wondered why Hopper was going up to Trinidad, the town up by the Colorado border.

Monk threw an empty beer can into the overflowing tub under the bar, then smiled, and Matt nodded, knowing it was his job to empty it.

Carrying the tub, Matt walked quickly down the alleyway next to the bar and dumped the empty bottles with one loud crash; he was not wearing his jacket.

Back at the door, he saw Marci coming on the sidewalk under the portico of the plaza, her hips switching from side to side, but he ducked into the bar door, feeling the cold coming through his shirt getting worse.

Marci's face was set hard, she was angry.

At the bar where Hopper had sat, Matt saw a man wearing a cowboy hat, and next to him a woman, the two of them wearing identical gold quilted jackets.

"I'll have a shot of Southern Gentleman and a Coors," the mad said tipping back his tan cowboy hat, watching as Matt set the tub down under the bar.

Matt, looking at the woman, asked over the clink of bottles Monk was making filling the cooler, "And the lady?"

"She just had a tooth filled," the cowboy said looking at her.

"We got orange juice," Matt said.

"Give her that," the cowboy said, watching as the woman pressed a handkerchief against the side of her face. "A small glass."

The woman nodded, and Matt poured her juice. Then as he took the bottle of Southern Gentleman with the picture of a mansion and a cart with tall wheels out front tended by two Negroes from the back bar, he heard a woman's voice say, "Would you care to donate to the cancer fund?"

Turning around, Matt saw a woman in a long brown coat and a knitted hat, holding a canister, standing behind the cowboy.

The cowboy did not turn around; he sat watching Matt pouring the whiskey into the glass.

The lady in the brown coat moved away.

Then when the woman with the canister left the bar, the cowboy said, "I'll give as much help as I got—when I needed it," and sipped his whiskey.

His wife nodded, sipping orange juice.

Marci was sitting on a stool at the end of the bar, and Matt went over.

"Everything set for your painting party tomorrow?"

"Elliott's wife," Marci said quietly with a pinched face, "has set up a meeting with her lawyer—just the three of them today. Elliott can't get away until after the conference. They're going to discuss—who gets what—if there's a divorce."

Matt had to force a straight face; he wanted to smile, and looked away from Marci at the bright stipe serape on the wall just above her shoulder.

"Tough luck," he said. "They had to pick the weekend for your party."

"Give me a drink, Matt,"

"What do you want?"

"A screwdriver."

Pouring orange juice into the glass, Matt glanced out the front window; the snow was blowing hard, he could barely see across the plaza.

Monk came up next to Matt, holding a plastic bowl of ice cubes from the back freezer, and said, "things are going to get slow tonight with this storm—maybe you won't need me."

Matt nodded, poking a plastic swizzle stick into Marci's screwdriver. "Okay, I'll stay until business drops off."

"You better tell Marci she can skip working tonight," Monk said grinning. "She's going to flip."

Matt nodded, looking at the four customers who were leaving the bar.

Marci made a groan, when Matt slid her drink on the bar in front of her, telling her she was not working.

"Shit," she said taking hold of the glass, "I wonder what else is going to go wrong today." After she took a drink, she said, "Hey this is strong—heavy on the vodka."

"You looked like you need it," Matt said.

"Damn—I like you," she said. "Let's go home and screw."

CHAPTER 6

"Quit putting on a show," Matt said quietly, while leaning forward on the bar looking at Marci's face. "Besides I got something serious to say."

At first Marci did not react, she just opened her large purse on her lap and took out a book of paper matches. Then she slowly tore the striking part of the matchbook off.

"Okay," she said, "let's hear it," her voice deep but with a hard edge. "So far today—has been a disaster, anyhow."

Matt watched her put the striking surface bit of paper on her tongue and bite down on it.

"The tally for the register," Matt said, "came up fifteen bucks short—the night you worked."

"And you blame me?" she said reaching for the swizzle stick in her drink, stirring slowly. "You think I took it?"

"Well, Monk didn't—and I didn't," Matt said looking up the bar where Monk was talking with two men sitting on the stools near the front window.

Matt was surprised she did not deny taking the money; she reached in her purse, took out some folded money, and handed him fifteen dollars.

Matt saw Monk looking when he put the money in his shirt pocket, then look away.

"I guess this means I won't be working tonight, huh, Matt?"

"No need," he said leaning back, looking at the front window and the blowing snow outside. "Business is really slow—but tomorrow night—might be different. We'll see how it goes."

Matt did not like playing bill collector; for some reason he felt Marci knew it also, and showed no hard feelings.

"My painting party is tomorrow night," she said sipping her drink; then taking a long drink added, "I'll be busy."

Matt nodded, feeling forgiven for the fifteen dollars. He liked Marci, he knew every part of her, including seeing the bridgework in her mouth when she slipped the bit of sulfur paper on her tongue, but he could not see himself married to her.

It made him wonder what Elliott saw in her that made him want to leave his wife and kids down in Santa Fe.

"Well," Matt said rubbing his shoulder, looking at the front window and the blowing snow outside, "I'm going to stay open until ten—snow or no snow—it's Saturday night."

When Marci finished the drink, she held out the glass to Matt, saying, "Could I have another of these—I need it, I'm having a bad day." She was lighting a cigarette, when Matt reached for the vodka bottle, and she said, "I'm going after this one—I left Elizabeth with the baby, and she wants to go over to her friend's house."

Matt was pouring a large vodka in her glass, and he said quietly, "I'll come over to your place—after ten. Okay?"

"Bring the vodka," she said. "The whole bottle."

After Marci left, the two men at the end of the bar went, after two more beers, and with no customers, Monk began tallying the cash register.

Matt watched until Monk turned around with the tally roll from the register, saying "Everything is set—all you got to do is take the cash out of the till and put it in the bag."

"Right," Matt said, and began washing bar glasses, while Monk, putting on his sheepskin jacket, walked to the door, then held the door open for two ladies coming in just as he was going out.

Matt started making two grasshoppers for the ladies who were regular customers. They came in almost every night for a drink after they closed the accounting office they owned two doors down from the bar. Nora, a blond was not too bad looking, Matt thought, but the other one, Frieda, was too heavy. Nora was just fleshy the way women get in middle age.

"I'm just having one drink," Frieda said as Matt set the drinks in front of them on small napkins. "Tonight is bridge night—we're practicing for the tournament next week."

"This storm just won't let up," Nora said. They were sitting at the end of the bar near the window, and she looked over Frieda's shoulders, out at the blowing snow. "It's been snowing all day—driving is bad."

Matt nodded and went back to washing glasses. He stacked the glasses, and wrote in the tab book the women only had one drink tonight; the women paid at the end of each week.

The door opened and in came Pablo, and his cousin, Hector, the local drug dealers, who everybody called, behind their backs, Mutt and Jeff. Pablo was short, and Hector towered over him, but was thin in an unhealthy way.

They both wore cheap suits, that fit baggy, and neither of them wore a coat, despite the cold.

"I'm just closing," Matt said to Pablo who walked down to where Matt stood behind the bar.

The two women stood up quietly when the two hoods came in the bar, and Matt saw them leave without speaking. They knew them.

"We don't want no drinks," Pablo said sliding on the barstool in front of Matt.

"I was just going to lock the front door," Matt said, wiping his hands on a bar towel, looking at the gaunt Hector, who was standing behind Pablo, grinning.

"We came for a loan," Pablo said slowly. "Maybe forty bucks."

"I can't loan no money," Matt said walking to the end of the bar, then around, crossing the floor to the door. "It ain't my money to loan."

When he reached the door, Matt said, "I'm going to lockup now. I'm going to ask you to leave."

The tall one slipped his hands into his suit coat pockets and stood grinning wide. Matt had heard Hector carried a foot long switchblade knife, so Matt stood watching him close.

"We can pay you back in a couple of days," Pablo said as he turned to look at Matt, swiveling on the stool. "Alex always makes us a loan—he knows we're good for it—he knows we'll pay him back."

"Monk took the money to the bank," Matt said, knowing they knew he was lying. "The cash deposit has to tally with the tape from the cash register. The money's gone—I can't loan you anything."

"Alex don't have no trouble," Pablo said standing up from the stool to look at Matt, "with no 'register tally.'"

"I don't know what Alex does," Matt said to avoid the loan, mostly because he did not like Pablo as a person, rather than the business he was in, "but I was told to put the money in the bank—so Alex could write checks—while he and his family travel—to cover expenses."

Matt had left the door unlocked so he could duck out quick if there was trouble. He had a plan to run across the plaza to the Sheriff's Office for help.

Suddenly, the gaunt Hector brought the knife out, and raised his arm. Matt saw the glint of the blade flash open.

"Bullshit," Hector said, his eyes wild, as he swung his arm down, sticking the knife in the flat wood of the bar surface.

"Hey," Matt shouted, "that's going to make a hole—I'm going for the sheriff," but when he pulled open the door, Hector's face changed quickly to concern. He took the knife, and deftly, with an open hand closed it and slid it in his pocket. "That's more like it," Matt said quietly, closing the door.

Pablo stepped in front of Hector, "Okay, we didn't come to make trouble. Okay?"

"I'm glad to hear that," Matt said pulling open the door. "Come back anytime—during regular hours."

Flakes of snow blew in from the open door.

"Yes, we'll come back later," Pablo said before he walked out the door. Hector followed without saying anything.

Matt locked the door, saying to himself, "I hope they <u>never</u> come back—they're too hard on the nerves—that was a close call."

Over at the bar, he looked at the hole the knife made, running his finger over the triangular slit, and shook his head, slow, from side to side.

"Those two belong in a cage. They're going to hurt someone—you can see it coming."

Turning off the bar lights, Matt put the cash from the register in the canvas bag, leaving the change in the coin sections.

He had to hide the bag or carry it with him; the bank had no night deposit set up. He did not want the responsibility of carrying the money, so he looked for a place to hide it. He looked at the empty cans in the tub.

The bottom of the throwaway tub had a crown on the bottom that left an opening underneath of more than an inch high.

"Nobody would think of the tub," he said lifting one side by the handle, sliding the bag under. "Not even Pablo."

He straightened up, looking around the bar in the dim light coming from outside in the plaza through the front window.

"Hope I'm right," he said and took the Smirnoff vodka bottle off the bar, pulled out the pour spout, took a quick drink, then held his thumb over the opening.

"Wait until Marci hears this one," he said going for his jacket. "She'll be more shook-up than I am." Putting on his jacket in the store room, then walking through the dark bar, he added, "If I knew I had to deal with those two psychos—maybe I would have told Alex to get someone else."

After locking the door, he walked quickly along the row of dark stores, out to the end of the portico roof that opened on the highway.

There was only a slow truck coming, so he skipped across the roadway into the alleyway drifted with snow, careful to keep his thumb over the vodka bottle under his other arm.

At the board fence in front of the famous art studio, he had to push hard, the boards of the gate blocked by snow.

At the door, he saw no lights inside.

"She must have went to bed," Matt said to himself. "Her daughters too—why not?—there's a blizzard going on," he said trying the door knob.

The door was locked, so Matt reached in where the cardboard was taped over the broken out window, and unlocked the bolt.

Inside, closing the door, he said in the dark, "Hey Marci, you got company," thinking she was sleeping on the studio bed, below the skylight.

In the dim light, he walked holding the vodka bottle out in front of him.

Someone pushed him from the darkness off to the right, making him stumble, hitting both shins against a low table.

The vodka bottle fell from his hand making a loud <u>thunk</u> on the floor.

"Hey," Matt shouted. "What the hell you doing, Marci?"

There was the sound of a telephone being dialed in the darkness.

"I'm not Marci," a man's voice said, just before the light came on.

Matt, rubbing both shins, looked up and saw Elliott standing over him in boxer shorts printed with a flying duck pattern. He was holding Marci's ashtray from the low table, the one shaped like a long fish, that she said she bought at the Hopi Indian reservation. Elliott held the fish at the narrow tail part, making it look like a club.

"What—?" Matt said straightening up. "What are—you doing here? The snow—the roads are bad for driving."

"The question," Elliott said, "Is what are <u>you</u> doing here?"

"I—was—invited," Matt said bending to pick up the vodka bottle. "I closed down the bar—so I came over."

"I just called the police," Marci said from the kitchen doorway, holding a blanket around her with both hands.

"Stay where you are," Elliott said hefting the silver fish ashtray. "You can tell your story to the cops, when they get here. When they arrest you for breaking and entering."

"You must be crazy," Matt said, holding the bottle up to the light to see how much vodka remained.

"You'll find out," Marci said, "you can't just go around breaking into people's houses." Her voice coming raspy, she added, "Unannounced."

"Bullshit," Matt said. "You said to stop over after I close the bar—and here I am." He tilted the vodka bottle, making the liquid drain out on the floor, "and here's the drink you wanted."

He started for the door, thinking of saying that Elliott being here, unexpected in this snowstorm, was the cause of all this trouble. Matt thought also he had said too much already, he was putting Marci on the spot for inviting him.

Suddenly, Elliot, pushed Matt hard, and he fell against the wall.

"Cut it out," Matt said not wanting to hit him.

Elliot, holding the ashtray with both hands, pressed Matt against the wall. Elliott was near the same height as Matt, but forty pounds heavier, thick arms and legs.

"You just can't come here," Marci said, her voice hoarse, "any time you want, Matt."

Matt felt sorry for her, her emotions were running high; he hoped he did not mess up her chance to get married—and whatever else she was counting on.

"Mother," came her daughter's voice from the stairwell to the loft, her voice high-pitched, "what's going on? What's all the noise?"

"Nothing baby," Marci said. "Go back to bed, honey—some people I know came by to talk—nothing important. Go back to sleep, and I'll be up—later," she crossed the floor talking, then stopped next to the bed. "Check the baby."

"Okay, mother."

A heaving knocking came at the door.

"Police!"

When Marci opened the door, Matt saw the policeman had the hood of his parka up over his head; he was carrying a long flashlight. Matt saw the policeman recognized him.

"Arrest this guy," Marci said pointing at Matt, the other hand holding the blanket close around her. "He broke in—and he threatened us. Arrest him."

Elliot set the fish ashtray on the table, and walked over to stand next to Marci, putting his arm around her.

"I didn't threaten—anybody," Matt said stepping away from the wall, his foot bumping the vodka bottle.

"Come with me," the policeman said.

Matt followed him out into the blowing snow, passing the door where the cardboard covering the broke out window was sticking straight out, the masking tape that held it in place, dangling like ribbons.

Outside, Matt, realizing the policeman was Pete Otero, an occasional bar customer, who someone said was a Korean War hero, did not know what to say. During the war, Otero had been captured and marched to North Korea in freezing weather to a prison camp, Matt had heard, and because of what he had been through in the war, nobody gave him a bad time.

"Get in the car," Otero said. "Front seat."

Matt climbed into the police car that had the motor idling, hearing the low radio chatter of the dispatcher.

"Where do you live?" Otero asked.

"Now?" Matt asked thinking for a moment. "Out at the Simmons' house. I'm managing the Pueblo Cantina—for the family. They went up to Michigan for a funeral. I'm running the bar—taking care of the house—for a week or so. I even have one of their cars."

"So you manage the bar?" he said nodding.

"Yep, me and Monk. Every morning I deposit the money in the bank."

A call came on the radio, and Otero picked up the microphone off its dashboard hook and spoke. Matt heard the words "Signal Seven" among the words the dispatcher said; a fatality.

"I even feed the cat out at the house," Matt said, not knowing what else to say.

"I've got a run," Otero said while hooking the microphone back on the dash clip. "I'm going to take you to your car."

"You mean I can go?" Matt said watching as they drove up the alley to the highway in the same track the car made coming in.

"Where's your car parked?" Otero asked, as they crossed the highway into Taos Plaza.

"Behind the bar," Matt said. "In the parking lot."

Otero turned into the alley next to the bar that was banked with blowing snow; he stopped, the headlights on the Chevy covered by a mound of white.

"Marci," Matt said to Otero trying to explain, "she asked me to come to her house—after I close the bar. I didn't know she had company."

"There's a lot of trouble at that house," Otero said. "Last time I was there on a call— some guy with a baseball bat—broke out the door window."

Matt, smiling, said, "So that's how it got broke."

"There was another guy," Otero said, "there, that time, too."

"Good thing she didn't call the Sheriff," Matt said opening the car door. "I might have wound up in the clink."

"All deputies are out patrolling county roads," Otero said, "looking for stranded cars."

"Well," Matt said getting out of the police car, "thanks for letting me off the hook—I owe you a beer."

"Just don't go back there," Otero said. "Tonight."

Matt slammed the door, grinning.

CHAPTER 7

When the police car backed out of the alley next to the bar, out into the plaza and turned, everything went dark in front of Matt.

He walked in the drifting snow in the faint light reflection from the plaza, then coming up on the Chevy covered completely, began brushing off the windshield with his hand. He could feel his socks getting wet from snow around his ankles, but before opening the car door, he stepped over to clear the back window.

Suddenly, he heard a dry scraping sound, then a muffled <u>thump</u>, as if something heavy fell.

Looking over the top of the car, he saw the dark figure of a tall man climb out of the window that was five doors away from the bar. The hardware store.

Someone inside slid a long, flat box out the window, and the tall man took it on his shoulder.

Matt ducked down behind the car, but kept watching. A second man came out the window, feet first, and dropped to the snow.

Each carrying an end of the box, they moved along the row of dark stores toward the highway.

"Mutt and Jeff," Matt said in a whisper, "taking advantage of the snowstorm." Opening the car door slowly, he dropped into the driver's seat. He sat moving his toes in the wet socks, hoping the two thieves were far enough away. He did not want to be seen; it could be fatal.

He sat a moment longer, hesitating, when the car swayed slightly. He turned to see the car blanket on the back seat rising in the dark.

Karen's face appeared in the dim light.

"Damn," Matt said, his hand in a fist, "you scared the hell out of—"

"I knew you wouldn't get in at Marci's," she said holding the blanket tight around her face. "I saw Elliott's Jeep parked next to the drug store. If he's over at Marci's—and you found out—you'd come back to the car."

"I thought," Matt said, relaxing, setting his arm on the back of the seat next to him, "the snow—the bad roads would keep him in Santa Fe."

"People in the drug store," Karen said putting one hand on Matt's arm, "were laughing about the roof collapsing from the weight of the snow—out there at that fancy house Elliott is building—for those rich clients."

"I'm not sure," Matt said, "if I should laugh or not."

There was a shuffle with the blanket, and Karen climbed over the seat to the front.

"I talked to Kozlo," she said slowly, "when I was home taking a shower and changing clothes. He phoned the house."

"They operate tomorrow, huh?"

"He's talking about not letting them operate on the back of his neck," Karen said running her hand over her hair to put it back in place. "I got to be careful—I don't want to get caught being someplace I shouldn't be—if he leaves the hospital."

Matt could smell the odor of scented soap coming from her.

"You really think he'll crash out of the hospital?"

"He talks like it," she said. "Let's go back out to the Simmons' house. It's nice and—homey."

"Nah, the roads are too bad," Matt said. "They're even worse than before." He looked at her face, white in the dim light, "I'm going to my room at the Romero's—I've had enough trouble—for one day."

He liked her, but he had the feeling Kozlo was suspicious she was seeing someone. If Kozlo kicked her out, Matt knew she would come to him—and he could not afford her.

He looked at her trying to think of a way to let her down easy—send her home.

"Let's go to your room then," she said. "If the roads are that bad."

"You had a tetanus shot recently?"

"It can't be that bad."

"It's unfit for human habitation," Matt said trying to say no to her; but he could not. "Writers can live in subhuman surroundings—and my apartment is no exception. It's where I do a lot of writing—and I have scant time for—house—keeping. It's a mess."

"You're exaggerating," she said and put her hand on his thigh. "Cut it out."

Matt started the car, hesitated, and then began backing up slowly. He felt trapped; he could not say no to her, and at the same time, did not want to say yes. Either way, it was trouble.

"Aren't you going to brush off the snow? The car looks like an avalanche."

"I can see out where the wiper is clearing the windshield," Matt said. "Besides, this way with the snow is better—nobody can see inside, see us together."

"I don't know whether to believe you—or not," she said.

"You—don't have a choice," he said. "None of us do—we—just kind of follow the carrot."

"What 'carrot?'"

"Never mind, Karen."

Matt drove slow on the road running west of Taos, to a cluster of houses huddled around the Romero compound, then turned through the archway in the high wall that surrounded the property. He parked at the corner of a low building where there were three apartments, separate from the Romero family house. Lights were on in all the rooms of the Romero house, and in the two apartments next to Matt's, giving the whole place a dim glow in the blowing snow.

Climbing out of the car, Karen, following Matt to the door, asked "Is this where you do your—book writing?" Not waiting for an answer while he was unlocking the door, she added, "so this is your lair—I'm curious."

"You asked for it," Matt said snapping on the light.

"Good grief, Matt, you need a decontamination crew—" she said slowly looking around, "for this mess."

There were yellow writing papers piled on the kitchen table near a typewriter, and more scattered on the floor. A stack of magazines sat under the table, mostly old issues of LIFE, mixed with travel publications. These were given away free by the Taos Library, discards from the files, offered to the patrons.

"I warned you," Matt said dropping his keys on the sink, which was filled with dishes, an upside down coffee pot on top.

"Do you have anything to drink?" Karen asked sitting down slowly on the edge of the unmade bed.

"I'm not sure—I'll look."

He reached down to the small refrigerator under the sink and opened the door.

"Ah-h, there's two dry slices in a cheese pack, half a jar of mustard, an open can of stewed tomatoes, and in the back—yep—a can of Hamm's beer."

"I'll take it."

"You'll have to share it," Matt said reaching in for the can.

Standing over the sink, while opening the can with a pointed opener, Matt glanced out the kitchen window. He could see the houses all lighted out back, the other side of the wall of the Romero property, were the wall was lower, as it followed the slope downhill at the back of the enclosure.

A flatbed truck pulled up and parked next to a house near the wall. Matt thought he saw the crook, Hector, getting water from that well last week and grinning, he kept watching. Then he turned off the lights to see better.

"What are you doing, Matt—turning romantic?"

He saw Mutt and Jeff climb out of the truck cab with the lettering Taos Fence Company on the door.

"Just being a nosey neighbor," Matt said before he took a sip of beer.

"Come over here," Karen whispered, "or I'll come over there—you're making me—excited—just watching you."

He walked over to the bed, holding out the can of beer, then stopped, standing in front of her.

She reached up, taking hold of his wrist.

"I thought you wanted a drink," Matt said pushing the rumpled sheets and blanket to the side, sitting down beside her.

When he kissed her, leaning to the side, she stopped him.

"No," she whispered. "You sit up, and I'll—sit on your lap."

There was the sound of a zipper opening quickly before she lay against him, her face against his. Then he saw only her throat; her head back when they began thrusting wildly.

*   *   *

It was near a half-hour later, when they lay together on the bed, when Matt reached for the beer can on the bed table.

"I'm hungry," Karen said, as if someone had told her she was, she not being aware.

"There's a few slices of cheese," Matt said turning his face to hers. "That's all that's here."

"I want," she said in a little-girl voice, "something warm."

He stepped out of bed, feeling the room warm now with the heat running, pulling on his Levi's, saying, "I'll look around."

In the cabinet above the sink he found half a package of hamburger buns, and made sandwiches with the cheese slices.

"How's a grilled cheese sandwich sound?" he asked her, feeling sorry she had to live like a servant to Kozlo; she seemed desperate and was looking for a way out.

"Super," she said sitting on the bed, pulling her sweater on. "Where's the john?"

"That blue door, to the right," he said while setting two sandwiches in a coated frying pan, turning on the flame of the gas stove.

Outside the window, movement caught his eye, and over beyond the wall, he watched as a tall man followed a short man, come out of a house near a well. Both men carried long packages wrapped in black plastic bags to the well rim.

Matt grinned watching Mutt and Jeff standing, looking down, pushing aside the rope that ran through a spoked wheel hanging from a frame overhead. Then Pablo hung over the edge, did something that looked like he hid his black package; he straightened up, and taking Hector's package, bent over, and hid it also.

A burning smell came from the frying pan, and Matt, using a fork, flipped over the cheese sandwiches.

Then, shaking his head, smiling, guessed there must be a niche, or crevice, just below the well opening. A perfect hiding place.

He watched both men climb into the truck and drive out of the yard.

"Something's burning," Karen said coming out of the bathroom.

*   *   *

The next morning, when Matt came around the bar building from the parking lot, he saw two police cars parked at the curb out front. Another car, with no markings, was parked over in front of the hardware store, where the county snowplow had cleared a parking spot.

Karen had gotten out of the car back by the Post Office so they would not be seen together. There was snow everywhere, but the storm was over, the sky clearing and people were digging out, Matt saw, looking around the Plaza.

Inside the bar, Monk was serving eight guys at the bar, so Matt walked quickly back to the storeroom without speaking. As Matt was hanging up his jacket, Monk appeared behind him.

"We need more Budweiser in the freezer, pronto," he said.

"Okay," Matt nodded.

"There was a big break-in over at the hardware store," Monk whispered. "The cops are over there now. They say half-dozen high-powered hunting rifles were taken—some with expensive telescopic sights." Monk began pulling at the side of his beard, "Guns like that—are worth a couple grand."

"Yeah," Matt said lifting a case of Budweiser bottles, "all that snow made it a prefect night for a robbery."

"Where did you stash the bar money?" Monk whispered, stepping aside so Matt could pass.

"Under the throw-away tub," Matt said quietly.

"No kidding?" Monk said, grinning, "I'll check."

Matt was putting bottles in the bar cooler, when he saw Monk lift one end of the tub, pick up the cash bag, wrap it with a towel, and set it on the low shelf under the bar. No one could see what he was doing.

Matt walked with the empty beer case back to the storeroom, and Monk followed.

"Pretty clever, Matt—hiding the cash under there," Monk said with a wide smile. "You ought to be a thief. You'd make a good one."

"I'll think about it," Matt said, "but right now I got to dump the empties-tub," grinning, putting on his jacket, he added, "before I trot over to the bank."

As if oblivious to what Matt said, Monk whispered, "See that guy sitting by the window, the one in the dark-blue jacket, he says he's a captain in the state police. I heard him talking to the guy next to him—they're looking for Mutt and Jeff—they want to talk to them, I heard him talking."

When Matt looked up the bar at the man in the blue jacket, and close-cropped black hair, he saw behind him, outside, Karen walking with a bag of groceries, crossing the plaza, going in the direction of Marci's house. He hoped there was no trouble with Kozlo—for her.

Then, before lifting the empties-tub, he counted the hard-boiled eggs in the basket on the back bar, and found five sold. He lifted the basket and took the five quarters and put them in his pocket.

He made a smug face at the mirror, before bending down to pick up the tub.

*   *   *

When Matt came back into the bar from depositing the bar cash in the bank, he saw Elliott sitting at the end stool.

Taking off his jacket, he leaned over the bar to Monk, whispering, "You serve Elliott, I don't want to talk to him."

Monk knew about Matt and Marci being involved, but not about the police being called last night, grinned and nodded.

Matt timed it, when Monk moved to stand in front of Elliott, he slipped behind him, as they talked, took his jacket off, set it under the bar, and began washing glasses.

Monk appeared next to Matt, and said, "He wants to talk to you. Be careful, we got five customers in here."

Drying his hands with a towel, Matt said to Elliott, "If this is about last night and the police—"

"No, no," Elliott said unzipping his tan jacket, Matt catching the Eddie Bauer label, when he slipped it off, "that's not what I came—to ask—"

"What then?—" Matt said quietly, "would—you like to drink?"

"A Cutty Sark—on the rocks."

"We don't have that brand. We have J&B."

"Okay. Make it a double."

As Matt was pouring the scotch, Elliott said, "I understand you're running the bar for Alex—until he comes back. And—I know—you help him—on a daily basis—clean up around the bar."

"Yeah," Matt said quietly, "I'm the <u>swamper</u> here—on a daily basis."

"Well, Elliott said picking up the glass of scotch, "I have a—proposition—a deal—for you, because your don't make a lot of money—you're doing some writing."

Matt had to fight to keep the grin off his face, looking at Elliott, dressed like a college student, tan corduroy pants, crew-neck sweater, even though he must be forty years old.

And here he was chasing Marci, leaving his family.

"It isn't—some kind of—crazy—deal?" Matt asked, standing, holding the bottle of scotch. "Something to be ashamed of—later."

Setting his glass down, Elliott said, "I know you don't have much money. And you like to drink—every—day."

"Yeah," Matt said setting the bottle down on the cooler below the bar, and leaned on his elbows, "I was a good customer here—spent a lot of time and money here—until my money ran out. Then Alex gave me the swamper job—mornings—for a couple of beers."

"And, I hear you have the hard-boiled egg—concession, as well."

"That came later," Matt said grinning.

"I'll give you a six-pack every morning," Elliott said, and lifted his glass to take a sip of scotch, "if you will keep away from Marci. You understand?"

Matt stared at him for a moment; thinking how was Elliott going to know if Marci was playing her part. He did not laugh.

"Yeah, okay." Matt said, "if you include a shot of Jim Beam," he added to make the situation more ridiculous.

"Okay, the shot included."

Monk came down the bar and took two hard-boiled eggs out of the basket.

"You better boil some more eggs later," he said to Matt.

CHAPTER 8

Matt poured another vodka for the young man with a crew cut, who had been drinking steadily for an hour. His two friends, one on each side, sitting at the bar, were drinking beer.

"I just got out of the navy," the crew cut man said. "We're celebrating—my getting out."

Matt, nodding, said, "Good for you," then set the bottle down on the sink, below the bar, to avoid a free drink request.

Turning for an instant, looking out the window, Matt saw Elliott, standing next to his jeep, talking to a man wearing a cowboy hat and boots. The hat and boots looked expensive.

Matt guessed Elliott was talking over there, across the plaza, earning his bread and butter from his wealthy client, and he grinned.

"Hey, is that a bottle of Saki down there?" the crew cut asked pointing.

Matt looked at the shelf on the end of the back bar and saw a white, slender bottle next to a white cup with no handle.

"Yeah, it's Saki," he said to crew cut, reading the label of the bottle, that was used more as a decoration, than an advertisement.

"Is it full?"

"No, half-full."

"Sell me the bottle," crew cut said reaching in his shirt pocket for money. "How much you want?"

Matt shook the bottle from side to side, "Well, it's a buck and a quarter a shot," he said looking at it.

"I was in Yokohama—for a while," crew cut said. "It will remind me of Japan—and some real good times."

His two friends laughed.

"Ten bucks," Matt said and set the bottle on the bar in front of him.

"Okay," crew cut said and took a bill from the money he held. "If you include that little cup too."

Matt set the cup next to the bottle, and went to the cash register; Elliott's jeep was gone from across the plaza, he noticed, and he had to smile, thinking of how Elliott was explaining the design of the building and the roof caving in to that wealthy client.

Just then Marci passed in front of the window, carrying the baby in the basket, her older daughter following pushing a shopping cart loaded with bags.

Marci put her hand on her daughter's shoulder, and then looked at the bar door; her daughter moved away, and Matt knew she was coming inside.

Hoping she was not going to start trouble, Matt moved down the bar to where it opened, in case she did.

"Matt," she said in her low-rasp voice, "last night was a mistake—I was afraid," she said resting the baby basket on the end barstool. "I been hearing—noises—outside my house—lately. I was going to come—get you out in the morning, drop the complaint—if they put you in jail."

"Okay," Matt said.

"I'm sorry I called the police."

"Okay," he said quietly, embarrassed by her apology.

She reached across to touch his arm.

"Elliott was so shook-up," she whispered, "he couldn't do nothing—after you were gone."

Matt looked away, wondering if the customers were hearing.

"I've got to get back to work," he said.

"Where's Monk?" Marci asked looking at the baby.

"At his girlfriend's house, doing his laundry."

"Kozlo's out of the hospital," Marci said. "Rather—he <u>walked</u> out of the hospital. He didn't want them cutting the back of his neck," she said. "So, he and Karen are coming to the paint party tonight. I bought a lot of stuff for snacks. I'm just going home—the party—starts—three, four o'clock this afternoon."

Matt stood looking at her, thinking the reason she was so easy to like, was she held nothing back—making her accessible; forgiving her for anything—was not hard to do.

He could not help wanting her. Everybody wanted her, and if she liked you, she was your soft companion.

"So, Kozlo broke out of the hospital, huh?"

"Ye-ah," she said looking at the baby's face, nudging the blanket down with a finger, "and he wants to do a painting. And I want you to come by too—and you <u>got</u> to paint."

"Well," Matt said looking over the bar, "after I close up—" he started, but stopped, when he saw Monk coming in the door. "I'm more a writer, than I am a painter," he said nodding at Monk. "But we'll see," he added to pacify her.

"I'm going to run," Marci said, picking up the baby basket, almost bumping Monk as he came down the bar.

"You come to my paint party too, Monk," she said stepping around him. "I'm expecting you both."

"All right," Monk said taking off his coat, "but I can't stay long. I got clothes in the dryer at Sylvia's house."

"No excuses," she said walking away to the door.

An hour later, only three snow plow drivers remained at the bar, when Monk said to Matt, "When these guys go, I'm going to lock the door—start doing the cash tally."

"All right," Matt said. "You going to stop by the party?"

"Sylvia asked me to hang around," he said. "Her twelve year old daughter—had a couple of moles removed from her neck yesterday. She's not taking the surgery stuff too well. Sylvia asked me to stick around—for help—morale support. She's taking it as hard as the kid."

Matt was washing bar glasses, nodding when he said, "I'm going to take the cash out tonight. I can hide it at Alex's house."

"He should be coming back by Monday or Tuesday," Monk said. "They should be showing up soon; he's got a business to run."

"I told Marci I'd stop by at her party," Matt said turning to see Monk counting the cash in the register, his back to the snowplow drivers at the bar. He grinned, knowing Monk was in a hurry. He had lied to Monk about taking the bar money to the Simmons' house. He had no intention of driving out there. He was going to go to his apartment, clean up, and go to Marci's paint party.

After they closed the bar, Matt drove to the Romero apartment, and inside, slid the moneybag under the refrigerator in the narrow space on the floor, below the electric motor.

When taking a shower, he held his head away from the spray of water to keep his hair dry. Changing to fresh clothes, he found only a sweatshirt with MICHIGAN printed on the front, was clean, and he pulled it over his head.

Driving slow back in the Taos Plaza, he saw across the highway two short lanes in front of Marci's house, packed with cars, parked every which way. He turned around and parked behind the bar.

Matt jogged on the sidewalk along the row of closed stores, hunching his shoulders, and stopped at the edge of the highway. Up to the north of town on the road he saw two sets of flashing red lights, police cars, and figured it must be a car accident.

Passing the parked cars in the alley to the Ufer house, there were a lot of footprints in the snow, all leading to the board fence gate at Marci's house.

Inside the house, there was a crowd, some sitting on the couch, some on the bed, others on the floor, all watching Kozlo, painting at the top of the giant canvas, standing on a step ladder.

The record player was blaring the Jackie Wilson song, "Higher and Higher."

Kozlo was painting a floating angel in a white gown; floating like a swimmer, and blowing a long trumpet. Below, was a village, the houses with thatched roofs, and sticks for fence slats, that Kozlo, now, was painting in, making sharp brushstrokes.

"Thanks for coming, Matt," Marci said. She was holding a can of Coors, and she was wearing what looked like a pair of jodhpur pants, making him smile. "What you think of my honored guest's painting?"

"Well," he said, lifting the can from her hand and taking a sip, "It would make a—good Christmas card."

"Hey," she said bumping him with her hip, "you're supposed to act—impressed."

"All right, I'm impressed, Marci."

"See that girl over there with the pony tail," Marci said in her low rasp, speaking to the side of Matt's face, "she's the one who painted the sunflower. She's an art teacher at the high school—"

"There are three of them—with pony tails."

"The one in the green sweater," Marci said. "And I heard she's a twenty-six year old virgin."

Matt did not say anything as he looked at the orange center of the sunflower with yellow petals radiating out.

"Maybe she's Rebecca of Sunnybrook Farm," he said smiling at Marci.

"Your spot," she said, pointing, "is there, just <u>under</u> the sunflower—and don't laugh. When Kozlo moves the ladder to the right a little, you can get started. The paints and brushes are already over there."

"Don't rush him," Matt said. "Let him finish," he added, welcoming the delay.

"Have another beer," Marci said. "They're in the ice in the sink—and I've got to run."

Watching her go, her rump in the tight jodhpurs, swaying, Matt caught a glimpse of Elliott standing in the kitchen doorway, talking with a young man and woman, the Dents.

Everyone in town knew the Dents; Caroline was crazy, and everyone was sorry for Brian, the young husband who had to go find his mentally sick wife, wandering in all parts of Taos, alleys, department stores, and even cornfields.

Most people knew she was not responsible for what she did, and called her husband, whenever she was seen out alone.

Brain worked for the federal government in a job that had something to do with soil conservation. He could not leave his job in Taos.

Matt knew all this, but it was hard for him to realize she was sick; he could only see she was slim, had large eyes, and long black hair that made her a beauty.

Looking away, Matt saw Karen talking to a middle-aged couple he recognized as the manager of an art colony that gave artists room and board free, as they worked on projects.

Matt had tried to get into the colony, but the man told him he needed a "recommendation" from the foundation headquarters back Philadelphia.

The wife of the Snitzer Foundation colony, stood next to her husband, smoking. Dressed in gray wool slacks and a cashmere sweater, with one arm folded across her middle, she was looking around, as if expecting some big event.

When Matt neared Karen, standing near the ladder, looking up, watching Kozlo paint with the manager-colony couple, he heard the man say, "Yes, it does remind one of Chagall's work—"

Matt, grinning about the comment, stood looking at his canvas space, next to a purple leaping frog, stretched out, and began thinking what he could paint in the spot.

Just then, he saw Marci come out of the kitchen door, her daughter following, eating a large taco, the napkin hanging down.

The teenager went to the doorway leading to the stairs for the loft, and disappeared.

When Marci saw him looking, she smiled at Matt, while wiping her hands on a towel.

There came a muffled <u>pow</u>-<u>pow</u> from outside the building.

"What was that?" Kozlo, turning on the ladder, shouted.

Then came a single <u>pow</u>, and a glass section at the top of the skylight, shattered, and fell to the floor. Women screamed.

"Somebody's shooting," Matt shouted.

Marci pulled open the front door, and people pressed behind her to look out.

"What's happening?" a man's voice asked.

Outside in the snow, a Sheriff's Jeep came up the alley and stopped. In the headlights, a man lying in a crouched position did not move, a splash of red blood on the snow next to his head.

"That's Hector," a man's voice said. "Is he dead?"

"Looks like it," a younger man's voice said, "Jee-ez."

Another Jeep with flashing red lights on top, turned into the crowded alleyway.

A Sheriff's Deputy stepped out and shouted to the two standing over the body, "There's another one—there were <u>two</u> in the truck—a short guy—"

The deputy kneeling next to the body shouted back, "Go back to where we stopped that white truck. Look for tracks—there must be tracks."

"I called for an ambulance," the deputy standing back by the second Jeep said. "The roads are open—they plowed the snow."

"Too late," the kneeling deputy said standing up, brushing snow from his pants, "he's dead—he was dead before he hit the ground. The bullet hit just below the right eye."

The deputy with him laid a blue plastic sheet over the body, saying, "A lucky shot."

"Who is it?" a girl standing with the party crowd in front of the board fence at the Ufer house asked softly.

"We're not sure," the deputy that covered the body answered.

"Let's go inside," a young man Matt recognized from the supermarket, who painted white birch tree pictures for tourists to buy, when he was not bagging groceries, said, "It's cold out here."

He put his arm around the girl who asked who the dead man was.

Matt was behind Kozlo and Karen going back into the house.

"I can't paint now," he heard Kozlo say. "The blood reminds me of Poland—back in the war."

"Somebody should cover that—all that blood," Karen said, her hand at the side of her face.

Inside, people were putting on their coats, talking in muted tones.

Marci walked up behind Matt, and said, "That was Hector."

"Yeah," he said without turning around, knowing her raspy voice. "And his partner is on the run."

He felt her hand on his rump; then she squeezed it.

"You're not going?" she asked. "You haven't painted your picture yet," she added when she saw him pick up his jacket. "I want to watch your bum—while you paint."

"Some other time, I will," he said putting on his jacket, grinning at her.

"Your spot will be there," Marci said grinning back, "when you're ready to paint it."

Looking for Elliott, Matt saw him pouring a glass full of scotch from a Black & White bottle over at the refreshment table.

"That's good to know, Marci."

Her daughter came down the steps, and Matt heard Marci say, "It was a car accident up on the highway—the sheriff is there," as she turned the girl around by the shoulders. "Now go back to bed—it's nothing important."

At the front door, Matt saw new putty around a glass put in the door window, where the cardboard square had been.

He opened the door, and saw the lights of the ambulance moving away up toward the highway.

"Nothing like a shooting," someone said behind him, "to bring a party—to a screeching halt."

Matt turned and saw Elliott; he held an empty glass.

"Yeah," Matt said, "things can get crazy sometimes."

"I wonder why he was in this alleyway?" Elliott asked, his hand on the door looking out.

"I never thought of that," Matt said. "See you around."

Outside, Matt said to himself, "That's a good question—why was Hector here—why this alley?"

Passing where the body had been, he saw somebody had kicked snow over the bloody spot.

Hunching his shoulders, he ran across the highway to Taos Plaza, and saw the white flatbed truck parked over in front of the Sheriff's Office with the Jeeps behind it.

Everybody at the party was shaken by the shooting, Matt thought. Except Marci, he remembered, passing the bar window. Then turning the corner into the alley, he recalled her coming out of the kitchen, smiling.

At the parked car, he stood unlocking the door, when he said, "Hell, she was on something—and it wasn't alcohol."

Someone stepped out of the shadows near the building.

"Take me to the Romero house," Pablo said; Matt stood for a moment looking at the machete he held at his side.

"Right," Matt said, feeling a fear that was like being hit in the face, suddenly.

They were driving on the road east of town, when Pablo said, "I know they shot Hector—is it bad?"

"A bullet just below the right eye," Matt said looking at the road, "finished him."

"Bastards," Pablo said, and was silent until they came near the wall around the Romero property. "Let me out here."

Matt stopped the car in front of the archway that went through the wall.

"Ain't this the first place the Sheriff will look?" Matt said. "They're going to tear your house apart—"

"You didn't see me tonight," Pablo said getting out of the car, keeping the machete low. "You understand?"

"Okay," Matt said.

When Pablo moved into the shadow of the wall, Matt drove the car through the archway, the lights out, and parked.

He sat in the dark, smoking, waiting until he felt Pablo was not close-by; he did not want Pablo to know he lived here.

When it felt like enough time had passed, he stepped out of the car, and slowly walked to his apartment door, unlocked it, and slipped inside.

He was glad the car was covered with snow.

CHAPTER 9

The next morning, driving into the bar parking lot, Matt saw Alex's Thunderbird; he nodded, grinning feeling a sense of relief they were back from the funeral and Alex would take back his duties of running the cantina.

Walking in the door, Matt held up the bag of cash and said to Alex behind the bar, "You want me to deposit this?"

"Nah," Alex said grinning looking over the top of his glasses, "I'll take care of it."

Matt handed the bag over the bar to Alex, and that was as close as they came to greeting one another.

Monk came from the storeroom when he heard the talking, and said, in a fake bossy tone, grinning and pulling at the side of his beard, "Hey, the empties tub needs emptying!"

"Right," Matt said, grinning, walking to the end of the bar to come around the opening. "Is the house all right?"

"Yeah," Alex said grinning at Monk, "but my wife is trying to figure out who—the woman was—that was in our bed. She says there's make-up on the pillow."

"How's the cat—Hitler?" Matt said avoiding the make-up comment. "He spent a lot of time alone in the house—when the snowstorm fell on us."

"He's all right," Alex said. "He ate all the Good And Plenty from the candy dish on the table—he must have enjoyed himself—we even found some half-eaten ones in the bathroom."

"That licorice is good for him," Monk said. "Clean him out—with the bubble-shits."

Just as Matt was bending to pick up the empties tub, Alex said, "I hear Marci's party ended with a bang."

"Yeah," Matt said reaching for the handles on the tub with both hands, "the Sheriff caught up with Hector—in Marci's alley—after—he heisted a flatbed truck."

"What about his sidekick—Pablo?"

"They're still looking for him," Matt said lifting the tub in front of himself. "The snowstorm is slowing them up, I guess." Alex walked the length of the bar ahead of Matt, and Matt said "I thought the snow would slow you up—it made the roads bad—I thought you'd be gone an extra day—or so."

"When we drove into Denver," Alex said, "we checked with AAA and they said the roads were cleared, so we drove down last night."

Alex led the way to the door and held it open.

"I hear they had a robbery at the hardware store," Alex said to Matt as he went by.

"Yeah," Matt said over his shoulder, "rifles."

* * *

That following Friday, a pool table was moved into the storeroom under a long florescent light hung from the ceiling. The fresh smell of new plywood hung in the air.

Matt was sitting on the row of cases of empty beer bottles that lined one wall, watching Alex shooting pool with a cowboy customer. Monk was out front, tending the bar.

"Pablo's mother," the cowboy said to Alex, "told the Sheriff that Pablo was down in Monterrey, Mexico, I heard." Alex had asked the cowboy if he heard anything and he was answering.

He was a modern cowboy, wearing a light-blue plaid western shirt with snaps, instead of buttons.

"He's got relatives down there," the cowboy said, shooting, sinking the four ball, "so, I guess, they're looking for him down there."

"He could be right here in Taos," Alex said after the four ball shot failed to impress him as much as the cowboy would have liked. "He has relatives and friends all over this town."

"Ye-ah," the cowboy said, chalking his pool cue, "who knows—for sure. They could be trying to throw the Sheriff off the scent."

Alex grinned looking over at Matt for a second. Matt had told Alex this morning when they opened the bar, that he had seen Pablo's mother, yesterday, carrying a shoe box, going to an abandon house near the well. Matt said it could have been a box of food for the fugitive son.

Neither Matt nor Alex wanted to be any part of the manhunt: there could be trouble with the law—or from Pablo's friends—if they said anything.

Matt had a clear view through his back kitchen window. He had watched two days ago when the deputies made a search with a dog around the well. But there were too many tracks in the snow, made by the people who draw water, for the dog to pick up a scent.

Marci came through the doorway to the poolroom.

"Hey," she said, running a hand on the plywood wall paneling, "this is nice—and it smells good too." She walked over to Matt on the beer cases. "This should bring in the customers—I hope it makes a fortune."

"It will take a while," Matt said smiling at her, looking at the short, synthetic fur jacket she was wearing. "Alex only gets two-bits—each time a game is played."

"It all adds up," she said, and then turned to Alex. "How was the trip to Michigan?"

"The girls didn't like it," he answered while leaning over the table to make a shot. "They got ant-sy. Too long a drive for them."

"How's Doris?" she asked.

"You can guess."

"Yeah. I see—and it's understandable," Marci said, making her voice drop lower, almost rasping. She took a moment to unzip her jacket. "I'm here to announce—Part Two—of my painting party—tomorrow night. Everyone is invited—except the police; and we're not counting on any of their interruptions."

"I'm not sure—" Matt began.

"You better show up," she said and pressed her stomach against his leg that was hanging over the edge of the beer cases. "You're not working as bartender anymore—and you're not going to get out—of painting your square on the canvas."

Matt could see by her eyes, up close, she was on something again.

"I'm really," Matt said quietly, "not much of a painter."

"Elliott," Marci said putting her hand on his leg "won't be at the party. His wife called him home—she wants a reconciliation, or at least time to talk about it. She says she's willing to overlook all the rumors she's heard—about me and Elliott."

Sliding off the beer case perch, Matt stood in front of Marci—so the others in the room would not hear, and said, "His wife <u>could</u> get everything in divorce court—you know. That would leave you and Elliott high and dry."

"I've been—penniless before, Matt."

"Alex," Monk called out from the doorway, "somebody out in the bar wants to talk to you." Then he whispered, "Cops."

"All right," Alex said, setting his pool cue against the wall near the door as he went out.

Matt looked out the door and saw two men in dark, wool suits; both with short haircuts, both the same height, making them look like twins.

"We are county detectives," the front one showing a badge in a folder to Alex behind the bar, said, "and we want to ask you about your car; is that your Thunderbird out back?"

Matt saw the second detective, standing behind the one talking, looking at the ceiling, then slide his hands in his suit coat pockets, and begin rocking back and forth.

They were not wearing overcoats, and Matt guessed they had run across the snowy plaza—in a hurry—from the Sheriff's office.

"Yeah," Alex said looking a little uncomfortable, "I own the Thunderbird."

"Do you always park back there—behind the bar?"

"Yes, usually."

"Our night patrol car reported a car parked there last week—the night the shooting happened over in the Ufer house lane. A report of a car all piled with snow."

"Wa-at?" Alex said. "I'm just back from a family funeral up in Michigan. That wasn't my Thunderbird—I was gone until last Sunday night."

"Okay," the detective seated on the stool said, nodding.

"I'm going," Marci said, walking to the front door, zipping her fur jacket, and smiling at the standing deputy, who looked down at the floor as she passed. They knew each other.

She went out the door, quickly, without looking back.

"I was parked back there," Matt said.

"Who are you?" the seated detective asked.

"Matthew Coates,"

"He ran the bar for me," Alex said, "while I was away at the funeral. He took care of our house—and we let him use my wife's car."

"It was <u>that</u> car," Matt said, "that was parked behind the bar the night of the shooting—a Chevy Caprice."

"Who's this other man behind the bar?" the standing detective asked, his hands in his coat pockets again.

"My name is Merton but people call me 'Monk.'"

"Are you a regular bartender?" the seated detective asked.

"No," Monk answered, pulling at his beard, thoughtfully, "I helped Matt out—doing the bar tally—at closing time. I used to work here—part time—before Alex bought the bar."

"Okay, okay," the standing detective, said, taking his hands out of his pockets.

"What time did you leave the bar last Saturday night?" the seated detective asked Matt.

"About ten o'clock," Matt said looking at Alex for a reaction, who was learning the details of what went on during the time he was away. "I closed because business was slow—the snow coming down heavy. Then I walked over to the Ufer house party to see what was happening."

"Did you witness the shooting?" the seated detective asked.

"We heard the shots inside the house during the party," Matt said in an even voice, "then we all rushed out to see what was happening."

"Then you saw the wounded man?" the barstool detective said squinting his eyes.

"Yeah," Matt said sitting down on a barstool. "We all saw Hector laying in the snow—all the blood near his head."

"After that the party broke up, and I walked back to the Chevy parked behind the bar, and drove home."

"You went to the Simmons' house?" the detective on the barstool asked, and taking out a small notebook from his coat pocket, began writing with a gold pen he took from his shirt pocket.

"No, I went to my apartment here in Taos."

"Where's that?"

"The Romero house. I rent a room out back."

"That's why Hitler ate all the Good and Plenty candy," Alex said grinning. "He was hungry."

"Who's 'Hitler?'" the standing detective asked.

"Our cat," Alex said.

The standing detective nodded, then looked up at the ceiling.

"Did you drive home alone from the parking lot?" the seated detective asked in a near menacing tone.

"Yeah," Matt said in a defensive tone.

"We found tracks," the standing detective said, "in the snow—on the passenger side of the car. They were smaller tracks—maybe a woman's footprints."

Alex broke into a grin, and then looked away. He knew Matt had taken a girl out to his house, and he knew it could not be Marci with Elliott in town. It might have been Karen, Kozlo's girl, he thought, grinning even more about Matt.

"Someone could have been looking in the car," Matt said. "Most of the day, I was busy in the bar."

"All right," the seated detective said while slipping the notebook back in his pocket, then the pen in his shirt pocket, "if you say you didn't have any passengers—we don't have any more questions. It could have been—anyone—looking inside the car."

Two young men came in the bar door.

"Hear you got a new pool table in back," one of the men asked. He was wearing a pea coat.

Then Matt remembered he was the guy who just got out of the navy, and drank the Saki to celebrate his discharge.

"Yeah," Matt said, pointing. "Right in the back there. The lights are on."

"You want anything from the bar?" Alex shouted.

"Two beers," the navy guy shouted, as he took off his pea coat at the backroom door, and then followed his friend inside.

"In just a minute," Alex shouted back.

The twin detectives were standing side by side now, looking like characters in a comic movie.

"We might have—more questions," the detective who had been sitting, said, walking to the front door, then pulling it open, added, "we might need to contact you Coates."

Matt nodded, and said. "I work here every morning—and I rent number three apartment at Romero's."

Matt watched them outside, crossing the plaza to the Sheriff's office.

Outside, the detective who had been standing during the interview, said, putting his hands in his pockets again, "Who the hell names a cat 'Hitler?'"

"Funny," the serious detective, stepping around a pond of water from melting snow, said thoughtfully, "those tracks only went up to the parked car. There were no footprints going away—from the car, the report said."

"You mean," the pocket detective said, folding his lapels over his chest, "whoever went up to the car—got in—on both sides?"

"Must be—huh?" the other answered.

"Anglos," the pocket detective said, "who can understand them."

"We better keep en eye on the houses in the barrio, behind the Romero place. Pablo's mother lives there. He could be hiding back there someplace," the thoughtful detective said, when they came to the door of the Sheriff's office.

"Or he might," the pocket detective said reaching for the door handle, "try to come and see his mother." Pulling open the door, he asked, "And how about this Matt Coates guy?"

"He's lying," the thoughtful detective said going through the door. "He might have given Pablo a ride home—or somebody else—the tacks prove it."

"Anglos," the pocket detective said, straightening his lapels, "you can't trust them."

"Yeah," the thoughtful detective said, "they're just like everybody else."

CHAPTER 10

That afternoon of the day he talked with the detectives, Matt finished typing Chapter Four of his novel, and he wanted to be with a girl.

He had written the pages of the story where the man character and the wealthy girl character attend the opera in Detroit, and he felt a rush of futility of going with her, she having everything, and he having nothing.

The scene he just wrote, summed up his own like, Matt realized, and he was bitter. Again he was bitter, when he chose the title, THE CARROT, THE STRING, AND THE STICK, when he started writing the book. He saw himself as a donkey following the carrot held out in front of him; the wealthy girl.

Today, he wished he had never met the wealthy girl in the Contemporary Literature class at the university. And, now to forget her, he wanted to be with a girl.

There was Marci. He knew Elliott was gone, and he hoped she was home. It was just after three o'clock.

Putting the six-pack of beer, that Elliott had bargained with him to stay away from Marci, in a paper bag, he walked on the wet road in the sun to Taos Plaza. The snow was melting rapidly, everywhere. He wished he had the car, but Alex took it.

Marci was home, and after drinking one beer each, the made love so violently, she made him stop.

"It's time to feed the baby," she said sitting up in the bed—"you—you animal." Pulling on a jersey, she added, "I love it—I love it."

She went to the small kitchen near the doorway, where the baby was in a wicker basket on the table.

"Were you ever married?" she shouted.

"No," Matt said, lying under the blanket, looking up at the skylight of the studio, seeing the light was fading outside. "I came close—once," he said. "But, I never did."

"You wouldn't have—any trouble," Marci said in her deep voice, "with—staying—married."

"What do you mean?" Matt said looking at the giant canvas on the wall across the room, where people had painted pictures in some of the spaces. "Hey, I don't really have to paint a square, do I?"

"Yeah, you do," Marci said making her deep voice, threatening. "Painting is an expression—of your—character, your thoughts. Everybody I know has to do it. Tomorrow is the deadline," she said; then there was a loud clank from the kitchen.

"I didn't get married," he said quietly, all of a sudden thinking of the wealthy girl, "because I wanted to travel—see London, Paris, Rome—and I'm not a painter—either. I'm a scribbler; I like to write stories. Maybe I'll be like Hemingway—live it up—to write it down, someday."

"Taos is more a painter's colony—than a writer's hangout," Marci said, before she spoke to the baby. "The—ere you are sweetie."

"Things really pile up on a guy," Matt said putting his hands behind his head laying in the bed, "when you try something like writing stories—on top of women and career—you have to make money—steady money."

"Money," Marci said, "is the—most important. If you have it, you can do what you want, even go where you want."

"Yeah," Matt said quietly, "that D.H. Lawrence guy who was here in Taos back in the twenties—he must have had dough. He must have made a lot of money on that 'Lady Chatterly's Lover' book."

"He wasn't much of a painter though—I saw those watercolors he painted, over at the hotel," Matt said lifting the beer can off the floor, drinking what remained. "Hell, a kid could paint that good."

"When he left Taos," Marci said, "Lawrence went down to Mexico. He wrote that book, 'The Plumed Serpent' about down there. Everybody around here still reads it."

"Well," Matt said, "he made money—from his writing, and that's what counts. I'm thinking of going to see Acapulco down there—if I can scrape up some money. It's supposed to be beautiful down there—and cheap," Matt said rising up on one elbow in the bed.

"So you never been married," Marci said in a tone that sounded like she was doing something; pre-occupied with feeding the baby, and was talking just to be talking. "I've been married—twice now."

"I know," Matt said lying back down on the bed. "You have two kids." He looked up at the skylight dark now. "I know."

"There's one more," she said. "A boy. He's with his father in Seattle. He's a year and a half younger than Elizabeth."

Not wanting her to tell more, smiling, Matt said, "Is she still mad at me for not letting her drive the car?"

"You were her only hope," Marci said, "for some road time. But the snow made the roads bad. You had a good excuse."

"Explain it to her, will you."

"Do it yourself, Matt."

"Okay," Matt said. "Okay." He thought a moment, then said, "while we're being honest—I shouldn't tell you, but Elliott tried to bribe me—to keep away from you." Matt smiled. "He offered me a six-pack—and I even conned him more for a shot of Jim Beam."

"Are you serious?" Marci said over the sound of tap water running; her tone was disappointment, disbelief and overwhelming interest.

"Alex said the same thing," Matt said pulling the blanket up over his face for saying it, "when he found the note Elliott wrote—under the cash tray in the register—and tore it up."

"Damn," Marci said from the kitchen doorway, "not even Elliott trusts me—that's terrible." She thought for a moment, and then added, "And you accepted the bribe?"

"How was Elliott going to be sure," Matt said, rising up on one elbow in the bed, speaking softly, "that we're not seeing one another?"

"Somebody is keeping him informed," Marci said. "Who put the note in the cash register?"

"It had to be Monk, Marci."

"So Elliott doesn't trust me," she said, absorbing the fact, "and <u>everybody</u> in Taos knows it. That's really a shock to hear."

"Look at is this way," Matt said, "he can't spend a lot of time here—because of his work in Santa Fe—and he's worried you might get—distracted—while he's away."

"A lot of guys have the same problem."

"He can go home," Marci said, "and screw his wife—and he expects me to live up here like a nun in a convent. That's men for you."

Matt smiled while trying to picture Marci in a convent. Then there came a hard double-knock at the front door.

"Now what?" Marci said walking to the door.

When she unlocked it, she wedged her foot at the bottom, so the door would only open narrowly.

"Pablo," she said, surprised.

"Is anybody else here?" he asked quietly.

"No, Elizabeth's at her friend's house. I'm just feeding the baby."

"Here's your three joints," Pablo said in an even voice, "but I got to have the fifteen bucks <u>now</u>. I need money."

He stepped inside, closing the door, but not pushing it shut.

"I got ten," Marci said, walking over and picking up her jacket from the chair next to the bed, where Matt lay still under the blanket. "There's two dollars and thirty-five cents, more," she said taking the money from the coat pocket, "and that's all I got. You're cleaning me out."

She threw the coat on the bed, surprising Matt, when it hit the covering over him, but he did not move.

"Okay, okay," Pablo said going back to the door with the money. "I'll get the rest—the next time I come."

"You'll get it—I'll have it next time," Marci said, putting her hand on the door to open it.

"Your boyfriend," Pablo said stopping at the door, "the guy with the Jeep."

"What?" Marci said looking at him hard.

"He was looking at a rifle in the hardware store—a couple weeks ago—one with a fancy scope—"

"So?" Marci said.

"Tell him," Pablo said putting the money in his jacket pocket, zipping it closed, "I know where he can get one like it—new—for a hundred bucks."

Nodding, Marci said, "I'll tell him."

"If he buys it," Pablo said, "you only owe ten bucks for the three joints—next time."

"Ill tell him what you said, Pablo."

"Don't forget, okay?"

"I won't."

"I need money," Pablo said backing out the door.

"I got to go back—to feed the baby," Marci said, while pushing the door closed. "I got to go."

Walking back into the studio, she added, "We all need money, Pablo."

Matt rose up on one elbow, and saw her going into the kitchen. He took a cigarette from the low table near the bed.

"No doubt about who took those rifles from the hardware store, huh, Marci," Matt said lighting the cigarette.

"I just hope," she said from the kitchen, "that the Sheriff don't think Elliott had anything to do with those damn rifles being swiped."

"Nah," Matt said grinning, "they already know." Putting out the cigarette in the fish shaped ashtray, he added, "Hey—you going to share those joints?"

"I'm saving them for the party tomorrow," Marci said from back in the kitchen in a faint voice. Then to the baby, "Tha-at's a good girl."

"Okay," Matt said, "be that way. Then come back to bed for a while."

"You better get dressed," she said. "Elizabeth is coming home—soon."

"This place is getting like a bus station," Matt said, half-kidding, throwing off the blanket, "with people coming and going." Pulling on his Levi's, he added, "It's time for my departure—I guess."

"Quit griping," Marci said, "you don't have—anything to complain about."

He walked over to the kitchen doorway, slipping into his jacket.

"Hey," Marci said wiping food from the baby's face, "where you going? I just said to get dressed—and that's all, honey."

"I got some stuff to do," he said at the same time the front door opened and Elizabeth came in.

"Hi kiddo," he said to her, knowing what was coming.

"I'm not talking to you," she said. "You don't keep promises."

"I'm not responsible for the snow," Matt said smiling at her. "Maybe later—after the snow goes—"

"I don't believe anything you say," she said while taking off her duffle coat, showing her pointed breasts under a pink sweater.

"Quit being so silly," Marci said. "Both of you." Then, when she saw Matt zip up his jacket, she asked, "You coming back later?"

"I don't know—for sure," he said. "Honest."

Outside, walking in the dark, trying to stay in the remaining car tracks in the snow, walking to the highway and the Taos Plaza beyond, all this was Marci to him, he thought to himself. Forever, to think of Taos, was to remember Marci.

She was this entire place, a caring mother too, and at the same time a sex-bomb, who will jump into bed with any guy she liked.

She held nothing back, even her personal problems and confidences. She spilled one day, he remembered, about what her doctor said after the last baby, about fitting her with an IUD device to avoid getting pregnant again, soon.

The doctor said, "My guts might come out," she said. "They're weak. He doesn't want them to drop."

Maybe, Marci was so willing, so available, that was why he liked her, Matt thought. She was easy to want. Guys like a girl like that.

Matt shrugged inside his jacket feeling the damp, so he walked quickly along the row of stores under the portico in Taos Plaza to the bar. Inside, he saw the actor Hopper sitting on the end stool, talking with Alex.

"This country around Taos is terrific," Matt heard Hopper say—"and the people are great. I want to come back here—after we make the movie. I might even settle here, buy some property."

When Matt walked around the end of the bar, both Alex and Hopper looked at him as if he was intruding.

"I just want to check the egg supply," Matt said quietly, while lifting the basket, then sliding the quarters into his hand.

"You going to boil more eggs tonight?" Alex asked.

"Not today," Matt said putting the quarter in his jacket pocket. "I've got to do some laundry—there's three eggs left."

When Matt was stepping around the end of the bar, Alex said, "Okay—see you tomorrow—morning." Hopper took a drink of his Mexican beer as if Matt was invisible.

"Sangre de Cristo mountains?" Matt heard Hopper say to Alex. "Why do they call the hills around here—that?"

"The blood of Christ," Alex said. "Yeah, in the evening when the sun shines—on the reddish earth—the people here think it resembles blood running down the hillsides."

"So that's why," Matt heard Hopper say.

Matt grinned, pulling open the door.

Matt walked to the Post Office on the west end of town. Checking the box Alex let him use for deliveries, he found a large envelope. His mother sent along all mail for him that came to his home up in Michigan.

It was getting darker as Matt walked on the road, wet with the rapidly melting snow, until he came to the archway through the wall at the Romero house; he had been thinking things were calming down around town, getting back to normal.

Walking under the arch, he saw all the lights, back, over the rear wall. The barrio houses and the well were lighted with floodlights, and there was the Sheriff's Jeep and two others parked near the well, and with the deputies, he saw a man holding a German Shepard dog on a leash.

"Somebody must have seen Pablo," Matt said to himself. "Or somebody tipped-off the Sheriff—where he was."

Watching, Matt saw Pablo being led out of one of the houses, his arms behind, cuffed, a deputy on each side. He wore only a t-shirt.

"Well, well," Matt said, "they caught the bastard. That ends that." Unlocking his apartment door, he stood watching as Pablo was put in the Sheriff's Jeep.

He watched until the lights were put out, and all the Jeeps drove off, then he collected his clothes, towels, and sheets, making a bundle for the laundromat.

Locking the apartment door, holding the bundle, he turned, and for a moment, looked over to the barrio houses, that seemed peaceful now in the dark, and shook his head, feeling a bit of remorse.

"He had a tough life, Pablo did," Matt said walking. "He tried being tougher—but it didn't work out." He smiled, shifting the laundry bag on the road back to town, "Maybe I can use Pablo in some kind of story. Ha."

At the laundromat, he sat reading a western magazine article about Kit Carson, who wanted New Mexico to join the United States, and when the dissenters tore down the flag in Taos Plaza, how Kit nailed it back on the pole, and sat, all night, his back against the pole, a rifle across his knees.

Suddenly, there was the sound of a police siren.

Matt looked out the window of the laundromat, but he did not see any lights or a car.

He shrugged. The laundromat was located on a side street, next to the supermarket; there was no view of the plaza, or the highway.

When the dryer stopped, Matt began taking his clothing out, putting it on a large table, when Arnold Hovey came in the door. He held a bundle of loose clothing, socks hanging.

"Pablo got away," Arnold said. "Can you believe that? He got away from the Sheriff."

"That's hard to believe," Matt said folding his clothes. "I just heard the siren—you got to be kidding."

"No, he's on the run," Arnold said setting his laundry down on the table, pulling off his overcoat. "He even took the Sheriff's Jeep—for shit's sake—can you believe that?"

"He won't get far," Matt said. "He can only go south, or north, on the highway—and it's patrolled." Looking at Arnold's rumpled sports jacket and tie, Matt had to smile; Arnold always looked rumpled when he came into the bar. "The side roads are all clogged with snow. He won't get far."

"Yeah," Arnold said stuffing clothing into a washer, "but Pablo's tricky—and he's got a lot friends around town."

When Arnold took out a handful of change from his sport coat pocket, he said, "My kid didn't tell me he had no clean clothes—for school tomorrow—until we were eating dinner."

Arnold owned the picture frame business that was on a side street near the plaza. The front room, of his house was the shop, where he had a work bench, and samples of all types of frames on display. He lived in the back with his teenage son, who was a little retarded. His wife died of cancer, he told Matt once, at the bar, where he was a frequent customer.

Folding a sheet around his stack of laundry, Matt said, "I wonder how Pablo got away? He must have been in cuffs, right?"

"I told you," Arnold said, "he's got a lot of friends around town—even in the Sheriff's department, you know."

CHAPTER 11

The next morning at the bar, Matt was walking in the alleyway after dumping the tub of empties, when he saw Elizabeth standing next to the bar door.

"Look at you," he said to her, swinging the tub by the handle. She was wearing a varsity jacket with a large T on the front.

"It's my new boyfriend's," she said, trying to be casual while pulling the embossed T out to look at it. "He plays football."

"I thought you weren't talking to me," Matt said smiling, moving toward the door. She stepped in front of him, and he stopped. "Maybe later, I can get the car again—and if I do—and Alex doesn't find out—you can drive it."

"Mom sent me over," Elizabeth said calmly, "and she said to say it is important." Looking away from his face, she added, "Mother wants you to come over to the house. She has to talk to you, after you get off work."

"All right," Matt said realizing something urgent was up, and holding the tub, swung it away to reach for the door handle, "tell her I'll come by—as soon as I'm done here."

"I'm still not talking to you," Elizabeth said, "and don't kid me about driving the car."

"Have it your way," Matt said going into the bar then added to himself, "your poor boyfriend—he's in for a lot of grief, I think."

Matt was walking the length of the bar to where the opening was, when Monk asked, "That your new girlfriend? She's a little on the young side—ain't she?"

"Marci wants me to stop by after work," Matt said while dropping the tub in its place under the bar. "Elizabeth is the messenger—that's all."

"Yeah, yeah," Monk said, continuing the kidding while wiping the bar in front of a guy, drinking beer, who worked at the gas station over on the highway, and who knew Marci, and was grinning. "You seem to be in big demand—over there—at the Ufer house."

"You could say that," Matt said quietly, not wanting the conversation to go on. Then looking out the window, he found relief: "Here comes Alex."

"They found the Sheriff's Jeep," Alex said wiping his shoes on the doormat. "Out behind the closed drive-in restaurant—south of town."

"Pablo probably hooked a ride south," Monk said. "Santa Fe—maybe, or even Albuquerque."

"Or he might have double-backed," Alex said, taking off his jacket, then straightening the eyeglasses on his nose, grinning. "He could be hiding right here—in town."

"The Sheriff's got a dog," Matt said, "and they could sniff him out—if he's someplace in town."

"They're probably checking that," Monk said. "Just to be sure—it sounds probable—I mean possible."

*   *   *

Matt knocked at the door of the Ufer house and opened the door.

Marci came out of the kitchen holding the baby, "Ah it's you," she whispered. "Thanks for showing up," she added, her low voice quivering slightly.

"What's the matter; what's the trouble?"

She rose up on tiptoes to Matt's face.

"Pablo is here," she whispered, shifting the baby so she could lean against Matt. "He's out in the shed—where the furnace fuel tank is."

"How'd he—get here?" Matt asked, his mouth staying open, as he felt the impact of what Marci said.

"The driver brought him on the fuel truck," she whispered. "He's a cousin of Pablo's, I think he said." Her voice broke. "Pablo wants to go to Mexico, I heard him say when they went back to the room, where the fuel tank is—the side of the house."

"Damn," Matt said, "this is really crazy—and it could get very dangerous."

"I know, I know," she said quietly in her throaty voice, "and I'm afraid for my girls—if the Sheriff shows up—guns—and dogs, and all that."

Her face looked like she swallowed something sour, then large tears rolled out of her eyes. She pressed against him.

"Okay," Matt said quietly, "take it easy." He slipped his arm around her shoulders. "I'll stay—until he leaves the house. Did they talk about—when—they were heading for Mexico?"

"I heard them talking," Marci said, wiping her face with the hand that was free from holding the baby, "and I think the driver said he was going for his van—but I don't know when he's coming."

"Well," Matt said, "Pablo can't wait too long. The Sheriff is probably checking around town—and they might show up here—with a dog."

"The driver told Pablo," Marci said, "when I heard them talking—that there's too much kerosene spilled on the ground in the shack. The dogs would not—get Pablo's scent."

"Yeah," Matt said unzipping his jacket, "that figures."

Marci, resting the baby on her hip, asked, "Maybe—we could talk to Pablo—ask him—"

"No-o," Matt said thinking, "we might be able to say—if he gets caught—we didn't know he was in the shack."

"The cops won't believe that," Marci said looking at the baby for a second.

"We got to say something," Matt said pulling off his jacket. "And we got to stick to it, once we say it." Dropping the jacket on a chair, he asked, slow, "What—time—did Pablo show up? How long ago?"

"That fuel truck came when I was feeding the baby—nine—maybe nine-thirty. I remember, I was surprised to hear it come alongside the house this morning—Elizabeth was having cereal."

"Where's she now?" Matt said walking to the kitchen door.

"School."

"Good," Matt said going into the small kitchen, then sitting down on the wood bench of the breakfast nook, at the same time Marci set the baby back in the basket on the table. "I think the van won't come until dark. We got to wait. Can you manage that?"

"Yes," she said tucking the blanket around the baby, "as long as it means—we can get out of this—safe."

"Good," Matt said, nodding at her compliance. "Hey, have you got anything to drink?"

"I made coffee just before you came."

"I don't need coffee."

"There might be a beer—one or two—in the back of the fridge." She opened a bottle and handed it to Matt.

"Are you <u>sure</u> there's a van coming?" Matt asked when Marci sat down on the opposite side of the table. The table was narrow, and high, Matt's chest pressed against the edge.

"I heard Pablo and the driver talking," Marci said, "when they were filling the oil tank—through the wall—talking. Later—Pablo came to my door and told me not to be afraid—through the door—that he was going to leave—when a van came."

Matt nodded, and then drank a sip of beer.

"So that's when you sent for me?" he asked.

Marci nodded.

"But why did Pablo pick this place?" Matt asked, holding the beer bottle in front of his face, waiting for an answer. "He has the whole town to hide in."

"I don't know," Marci said, then taking the beer bottle from Matt's hand, took a quick drink. "I don't know," she said. Giving him the bottle back, then standing up, "I'm hungry," she said slowly. "All I know—from them talking—the driver was flagged down by Pablo—on the highway, south of town, near the A&W drive-in that's closed. The driver was coming here—that's Pablo's cousin—to fill the damn tank—on a back order."

She put a frying pan on the stove.

"What you doing?"

"I'm going to grill some hotdogs," she said opening the refrigerator door. "How many you want Matt?"

"Two, I guess," he said and took a drink from the bottle, watching her break away the frozen hot dogs from the pack. "But why here, Marci? What brought him here—of all the places—?"

"Maybe he feels I won't tell the police—or the Sheriff," she said, in a low voice from the back of her throat. "Or something—like that. And—he told me—he'd give me two joints a week—free—for keeping quiet."

Smiling, Matt felt the satisfaction of getting the answer out of her. He knew she was hiding something about Pablo.

He watched her roll the hot dogs into the pan, then add bacon grease from a can on the side of the stove. There was a crackling noise.

"How many weeks," Matt whispered. "How many weeks is Pablo going to give you the joints?"

"Nobody likes a smart-ass, Matt."

"You know you could go to jail," Matt said. "It's a crime to—hide a fugitive from the law."

"Be quiet, Matt. Talk about something else," she said slowly in her raspy voice. "He might be listening."

"What about," Matt began, "the paint-party, tomorrow night?" He was smiling, talking to appease her. "What if he's still in the fuel room back there?"

"We'll just have to have the party," she said taking plates out of the cabinet.

They were eating the hotdogs, wrapped in a slice of bread that was spread with mustard, when Marci said, "What about you—you being a fugitive? Some people here think you're on the run—from something." She licked the mustard off her thumb. "They say you don't fit—in an artist colony. There's been some talk, Matt."

"Maybe," he said and finished the beer in the bottle.

"What you mean, 'maybe?'"

"I'm not sure," he said, putting the remainder of his hotdog on the plate, then sitting back.

"Is someone after you, or not?"

"Yeah, the army maybe—or some other department in the government."

"What'd you do?" Marci asked opening the last bottle of beer, sitting back down at the table, then taking a sip, and watching Matt for an answer. "You didn't steal the army payroll—or something like that?"

"No, it was a disease I had," he said lifting the can of VanCamp's beans from the table. He took a spoonful out of the can, and then swallowing, said, "I kept complaining I didn't feel well, but the German doctor at the dispensary, there in Wurzburg, said I wasn't sick.

"I'd gone to the dispensary—three, four times—and that doctor said if I kept it up, he was going to report me for malingering."

"So what happened?" Marci asked, reaching for the can of beans. "Don't stop," she said taking a spoonful, "tell me what happened next."

Matt watched her put the spoonful of beans in her mouth, her eyes wide, looking at him across the table. She was exited.

"When I got leave a couple weeks later," Matt said taking a quick sip of beer, "I went to the big Army hospital in Frankfurt—and I asked for an x-ray."

"What did the x-ray show, Matt?"

"I had TB," Matt said, shaking his head, "in the advanced stage. In fact, the Colonel-Doctor who I talked with when they put me in the hospital, told me, 'If you would have waited a few months longer—we would not have been able—to do anything for you.'"

"Wow," Marci said, putting her hand on his, "you were right—all the time. Weren't you? And it saved your life."

"Yeah," Matt said leaning back, "but some of the other guys in my outfit caught the disease—from me, I guess. The Army had them x-rayed—even some of the officers in my unit."

"I see," Marci said. "And now—you think the Army is after you, for all that trouble?"

"Could be," Matt said, leaning down on the table. "They might think I'm some sort of spy—that spreads diseases—something along those lines."

"And you're not sure—about any of this?" Marci asked.

"It sort of comes and goes," Matt said. "Odd things happen to me—and I get a feeling that what happened—was deliberate—not just a coincidence."

"Ah, I get it," Marci said leaning on the table looking at his face, "and you think all this odd-happening stuff is—caused—by someone following you around?"

Matt just nodded.

"Yeah," he said finally, "I guess it sounds silly—maybe even—sick."

"I don't think you're sick, Matt. And I'm sorry I asked you—about this stuff, and I'm going to keep it to myself."

The front door opened, and Elizabeth came in.

Marci stood up, her hands on the table, leaning forward, and in a whisper, said, "Some people around town think you're some kind of 'plant,' an investigator—be careful. They might try something—be careful." Going to the kitchen door she said to her daughter, "How come you're home so early?"

Matt heard Elizabeth say, "I broke up—with my boyfriend—Carlos."

"No pizza and the movies tonight, huh?" Marci asked.

"Uh-uh," Elizabeth said, then Matt heard her ask, "what those guys with the van doing to our oil tank—they're parked by the side of the house?"

"They're fixing a—a leak, honey," Marci said as the two of them came into the kitchen. "They filled the tank earlier today—and they found a leak—so they're fixing it."

Elizabeth looked at Matt for a second, and then looked away.

"We didn't hear the repair van," he said to her. "We were eating—we didn't hear them drive up."

Elizabeth, unzipping her jacket, said, "You think they'd at least knock on the door—tell you they were here, when they drove the van up. They're using flashlights out there in the room where the tank is."

She was suspicious of who was working in the tank shed; Matt looked at Marci, but did not speak.

"Could be," Marci said sitting back down in the nook, across the table from Matt, "they knocked on the door—but we didn't hear them."

"Yeah," Matt said in an effort to stem Elizabeth's suspicion more, "we were telling our life stores. Heavy stuff."

Elizabeth knew Matt and her mother spent nights together before, and she looked up at the ceiling turning away, and went out the kitchen door slipping off her lavender quilted jacket.

"I'm beat," she said from the other room. "I'm going to lay down up in my room."

"Honey," Marci said, "take the baby upstairs with you. It's drafty down here."

"Okay," Elizabeth said and came back, then lifted up the baby in the basket off the table, and added, "It's sort of spooky—those flashlights."

Matt was trying not to let her see him looking at her pointed breasts.

"We'll be here until they go," Marci said. "Matt and I will be right here until they get in the van and leave."

Matt added, "You might hear the van go soon, they probably won't be much longer."

He was trying to reassure Elizabeth like Marci was.

When she walked out of the kitchen carrying the baby basket, Elizabeth turned suddenly to look back; she caught Matt watching her rump, by making eye contact.

He looked away quickly.

"They can't leave soon enough," Marci said in a low, gravely tone," as she stood up from the table. "Help me clear the table Matt," she said picking up the two plates. "Cimarron is on television in a few minutes. We can watch it out in the studio."

The skylight windows had changed from a light blue to a darker shade now, Matt noticed, when they came out of the kitchen. He snapped on the television set.

Marci sat down next to him on the couch, pulling a brightly stripped Mexican blanket, that had covered the back of the seat, over herself.

Then the rolling-scraping sound of a door being closed in the van, came, followed by a thump, out at the side of the house.

"They're leaving," Marci said as the drone of the truck motor faded. "We're off the hook."

"Sounded like it," Matt said, watching the western TV program. He had a hard time imagining the English actor, Whitman, as a cowboy, and was losing interest. He liked the name Cimarron; the name of a river up north of Taos. He liked to say it.

"Mom?" came Elizabeth's voice from the top of the stairway, "I heard the plumber's truck go."

"Okay, honey," Marci said sitting up straight to shout. "We heard it too—you can go to sleep, everything will be quiet, now."

"I'll be up to check the baby—'soon as my TV program is over."

"All right," Elizabeth said from upstairs, walking, making the boards creak.

"I need a drink," Matt said, as Marci was settling back under the blanket beside him. "Think I'll take a walk—down to the bar."

"Stay a while longer, Matt. Stay until the program is over—stay to the end."

"I feel—edgy—and I need a beer," he said looking at her, feeling his usefulness was over, now that the van was gone.

"You drink too much, honey," Marci said, putting her hand on the side of his face. "It's got a hold on you—you could end up in the alcoholic ward of some hospital—if you keep going the way you are."

"I'm going to go for—" he began, while sitting up.

Marci wrapped an arm around his neck, pulling him back. There was the sound of a zipper opening.

CHAPTER 12

Alex Simmons knocked at the door of Matt's apartment. The sun was rising over the hills to the east, and Alex turned, grinning and sliding his eyeglasses up his nose, aware Matt was hung-over, smiled at his wife, Doris, and her two girls, sitting in the Thunderbird.

"Time for <u>our</u> mystery trip," Alex said turning to the apartment door. "You said you wanted to go to last night at the bar—and here we are."

"I can't go," Matt said in a low voice. "I'm—too sick."

"You didn't stop someplace?" Alex said grinning wider. "I mean—after you left the bar?"

"I—went to the Frame Shop," Matt said.

"Ah-h," Alex said looking at the water dripping off the edge of the roof just over his head, "you and Arnold belong on the Olympic drinking team."

After the sound of being unlocked from the inside, the door opened a few inches.

Alex, pushing the door open wider, asked, "What did you guys have to drink?"

"Wine," Matt said, standing next to the bed, both hands covering his face, wearing only briefs. "And I'm sick—as a dog—I have to—sleep. I want to sleep."

"You only had a few beers last night before you left," Alex said looking around the room, and over at the pile of note papers on the table by a typewriter.

This was the first time he saw how Matt lived, away from the bar, and he grinned.

"We drank—a lot of wine."

"You shouldn't be that—hung-over—with just wine."

"Arnold remembered—he had a pint of gin," Matt said, slowly, sitting down on the side of the rumpled bed. "I think I'm on fire—inside," he said looking at the floor. "And my head has a buzz-saw running in my brain, trying to come out."

Alex handed him a can of beer from his pocket, "Hey, it looks like you've done a lot of writing—all these papers."

Matt opened the can and drank some of it.

"Yeah," Matt said pausing, looking at the can, "I'm just finishing the eleventh chapter," and he sat up. "I need to skip the 'mystery trip' today—I'm too—sick."

"C'mon—get dressed, Matt—the women are out in the car waiting."

When he finished the beer from the can, Matt said, "I need—another drink. Give me a break."

"I am giving you a break," Alex said. "Get dressed. Doris has a thermos of coffee. You'll be glad—you'll see I'm right—this trip is worth the effort."

Doris was sitting up front in the car, her early stage of pregnancy showing. The two girls were in the rear seat, and when Matt climbed in the back, they were not happy about the crowding, and made faces.

Matt sat with his knees against the back of Doris's seat.

"You look hung-over," Doris said. "Where'd you end up last night? You only had a few beers before you left."

Matt, looking at the side of her potato shaped face, while she was talking, wondered what Alex saw in her. She had been in the bar, last night, one of the few times she came to study the family's business. She would watch the customers, and make sharp comments about people to Alex, as he passed, serving them. She always perched on the stool at the end of the bar.

"I went to the Frame Shop," Matt said quietly.

"Oh-h," she said, "so you and Arnold teamed up—'bird's of a feather.'"

"Gin with wine chaser," Alex said driving, looking in the rear view mirror, grinning widely.

"That explains everything," Doris said looking forward.

Matt pulled his jacket collar up, around his face, and slouched in the cramped back seat.

"I'm going to sleep," he said. "Pick up where I was before—I was interrupted."

"It's worth the trouble, Matt. You'll thank me later—for rousting you out."

"Okay, okay," Matt said. "As long as we get back for Marci's paint party tonight."

"When do you find any time to paint?" the youngest of the girls asked. She was sitting next to him.

"I'm not a painter," Matt said in the tone of an angry parent, "I'm a writer—I'm writing a book. That's why I came to Taos."

He turned to look at the girls. Neither of them were good looking. They were just younger versions of Doris and her first husband.

"What's the name of your book?" the older girl asked, turning away from the window to look at Matt, her brown hair falling on the side of her face.

"The Carrot, The String, and The Stick" is the working title of the novel," he said calmly, like a teacher.

"What's it about?" the younger one asked.

Matt sensed everyone in the car waiting for his answer.

"It's about a guy who meets a rich girl—in college," Matt said trying to make it sound interesting. "And the girl's father—does everything he can to break them apart—but they guy fights back. He's like a donkey, following a carrot, hanging on a string from a stick, held out front of him." Matt exhaled, and added, "He can't let her go."

"That's sad," the older girl said.

"How does it end?" the younger girl asked while scratching her knee. "Does the guy get the girl?"

"Uh-huh," Matt said, "they get back together—in the end."

He did not want to list the tragic details of the ending. It was hard to tell the whole story in a few words, so he left out details in his summary.

But he did say, "Yeah, the father of the girl—and maybe the Feds—worked to break up—the romance."

"Why does the guy think the Feds are involved?" Alex asked looking at Matt in the rear view mirror.

Realizing everyone in the car now was interested in the story; and Alex sensing it was a biography that was being told, Matt spilled what he told Marci before, about his novel.

"They guy was in the army—Germany—and he caught a serious disease. Some of the other soldiers in the guy's outfit contracted the disease. The army began to investigate over in Europe—to see if the guy was some sort of spy—who spread diseases."

"And back in the United States—the investigation continued, when the guy returned home, and got out of the hospital."

"I like the beginning of the story," they younger girl said, "but I don't like the spy stuff."

"Why would the Feds break up these two lovers?" Alex asked, knowing Matt was telling his story of life before he came to Taos.

"The Fed investigating they guy—is young—and he falls for the girl," Matt said, "and the wealthy father approves of him."

"The Feds wouldn't do that," Doris said. "That would be illegal, wouldn't it?"

"Who's going to know?" Matt said. "The Feds won't say anything—and after the wedding—it's too late."

"What does the girl think?" the older girl asked.

"What woman can resist a marriage proposal and a ring?" Matt said quietly. "Following a father-approved whirlwind courtship. It started when the father wanted her 'to see other people.'"

Everybody in the car was silent, thinking about the story Matt told, as they drove through Santa Fe with its historic adobe storefronts.

"There ain't much snow left down here," the older girl said, her face to the window.

"Hey Alex," Matt said, "how much further—I got to go to Marci's party tonight?"

"Not much further," Alex said being sympathetic with the story Matt told. Turning to Doris, he added, "Give Matt some coffee, honey. Something to settle his nerves."

"Am I being shanghaied?" Matt asked when taking the coffee cup from Doris over the seat. They were driving west now. "I thought we were going to see where Billy The Kid was shot by the Sheriff—or something like that."

"Relax," Alex said, "enjoy the ride."

Matt, clutching the plastic coffee cup in front of his face, looked out at the flat country, that was mostly desert, they were driving through now, and shook his head.

"Good thing it's cloudy," Matt said after sipping coffee, "we don't have the bright sunlight blinding us."

No one spoke.

"I don't see how," the oldest daughter said, "the rich girl could get engaged—if she still loved the student guy."

"She broke off the engagement," Matt said looking into the empty coffee cup, "and the college kids get back together."

"Well," the younger girl began, "how did the rich girl get married to the—investigator creep?"

"The father talked to him," Matt said. "Told him to propose marriage and offer a ring. The father—then put pressure on his daughter—to accept the offer. The investigator even cried when proposing."

"I don't see how the investigator," Doris said, "knew all this stuff."

"He, and other investigators," Matt said handing the cup back to Doris, tapping it on her shoulder, "had been following the college kids. Wherever they went, the cafeteria, library, even to a bar, an investigator was always near—listening."

"It don't sound—legal," Doris said, turning, taking the cup. "I mean to pry into the kid's—private life."

"It was done—for government security," Matt said. "The investigators were keeping the country safe—is what they would say—legally."

"It's going to take you a—hundred years—to write all this stuff," the youngest girl said. "To get all that into your book."

"I can't wait to read it," the oldest girl said. "Hurry up and finish writing it. I want to see how the book ends."

"I'm writing as much as I can," Matt said. "I'm almost half-way done with the first draft." They were passing a closed, old style gas station with the paint peeling off the walls. "Hey," Matt said smiling, "we're on old Route Sixty-Six—for Pete's sake."

"Yeah," Alex said, "it goes all the way to California."

"I promised Marci," Matt said, "I'd show up in time for her party—Part Two."

"You'll be there in time," Alex said, not kidding now.

"Hey," the older girl said, "there's no snow down here at all—that's funny."

"It's the wind," Alex said. "It's so strong."

"There's Albuquerque," Doris said pointing, "up ahead in the distance."

"Don't the boy and girl in the story," the youngest girl asked, "get back together—by the end of the book?"

"Ah-h, yes," Matt said.

"How can she," the oldest girl asked, "she's married to the investigator guy?"

"She leaves him," Matt said. "Then her father is angry, and her husband—is angry too."

"Then how does it end?" the younger one asked. "I'm worried."

"I'm not sure," Matt said. "I haven't worked out the denouement exactly—the ending."

"If the girl in the story leaves that husband," Doris said, wiping out the coffee cup with a Kleenex, "it serves that rat—the investigator, right."

They were driving through downtown Albuquerque.

"How far west we going?" Matt asked. "San Diego?"

"Relax," Alex said, grinning, pushing his eyeglasses up on his nose, "we'll be there in a—few—I've got to stop in a while."

"Why," Doris said looking out her side window, "does the investigator guy in your story Matt—why is he from New York?"

"Yeah," Matt said, shifting his legs against the back of Doris's seat, "that's why they guy in the story thinks he's a fed investigator. The girl tells the guy stuff about the background of this guy she met in class—and the stuff he tells her—don't add up—it's all full of holes about Detroit. Then he says he's the son of a stockbroker in New York—a wealthy stockbroker."

"Oh, man," the younger girl said, "I can't wait to read this book—I want to know how the story works out—I'm dying."

"For some reason," Matt says, after the investigator marries the girl—they move to New York City—so the college guy in the story, thinks the guy is an investigator from the New York Fed office. And to boot—he looks like a movie star. He looks like that Horst Buc—in the "Magnificent Seven" western movie."

"Why did they send him—Buch-holtz—to break-up the college kids? A guy from New York," the oldest girl said looking at Matt next to her, "comes to break-up—or investigate—college kids in Detroit?"

"I think," Matt said, "originally, they want to bust the college kid's hump—make him suffer—take his girl away. But, the New York guy falls for her himself. Who wouldn't—she's a knockout and wealthy."

"Don't tell any more," the youngest girl said looking over at Matt, "I can't stand any more—complications."

"I don't understand," Doris said, "why they have to investigate the college kid—in the first place."

"The disease thing," Matt said. "They think he's a spy who spreads diseases. They want to destroy him."

Matt saw Alex look at Doris for a moment, as if to say, that was the reason Matt came to Taos. He's a fugitive.

"Can't this college guy in the story," Alex said looking at Matt in the rearview mirror, "go to the Inspector General of this federal department—make a complaint?"

"Nah," Matt said. "They claim they're defending the country against all enemies—foreign and domestic. That just about covers everything they do."

"I understand," Alex said. "They have a blank check."

"Yeah," Matt said. "They can do pretty much what they want—and they're covered."

"Maybe the girl," Doris said slowly, "just met a new boyfriend—in class at the college." Matt did not answer.

They were travelling in desert country now, and in the distance there were outcroppings, as high as skyscrapers. They had once been volcanoes, now they were stone monuments, reddish, standing where the sand had been blown away around them by centuries of wind.

"So this is what we came out to see," the oldest daughter said, her face against the car window. Then turning to talk to the back of Alex's head, she added, "Some 'Mystery Trip.'"

"The sign over there," the younger daughter said in a similar tone of disappointment," says ACOMA. What's at Acoma?"

"There's an Indian tribe," Alex said, "that's lived up top of this outcropping for centuries—and we're going up for a look-see."

"It looks like a fortress—or a castle," Matt said, looking out the car window at the outcropping, the former core of a volcano that rose to several hundred feet.

The youngest daughter, reaching across her sister, rolled down the car window to look up.

"You mean we're going—way up there?" she asked, her head out the window.

"Yes, Barbara," Doris said to her, watching as she looked out the window. "That's why your father brought us here."

"He's not my father," she said bringing her head inside.

"Legally, dear, he is your father," Doris said flatly.

"How we going to get up there?" the older girl asked. "We don't have to climb—do we?"

"They just finished making a road up," Alex said. "They just opened it to the public. It's around the other side."

"Look at the size of this rock," the older girl said. "They could hide a whole city—up there."

"Yes," Alex said, "it's a geologic phenomenon that supported life up there for centuries."

"It's a monolith," Matt said, "formed by liquid magma that rose up from the center of the earth and solidified."

"Did you study geology at college?" the oldest girl asked.

"I had a class," Matt said, "and I really enjoyed learning all the geologic categories—geodes, crystal formation and the old stuff formed back in pre-historic times—trilobites. If you go to college, I hope you enjoy the class as much as I did."

"College," the youngest girl said, "she'll be lucky to graduate from high school."

"Hush, now Barb," Doris said. "No need to be nasty."

"This is exciting," the older girl said. "It's like exploring."

Turning off the highway onto the Acoma Indian Reservation, Alex stopped, and was paying the man at the gatehouse for the road up to the top, when he said, "I can hardly wait to see the view from up there. I've been reading a guide book about this place."

Driving up the steep road of new tarmac, Matt saw workers still jackhammering away rock outcroppings near the passageway. It grew dark as they drove up slow; Alex had to shift the car into a lower gear. No one spoke as they passed along the tall walls.

Then, at the top, they came out into the light again.

"Look," the older girl said, "they got a cathedral over there."

Matt sat silent, feeling a sweep of remorse for talking about his geology class at the university. It brought up the feeling he was being watched. There had been a guy at the class worktable, he remembered, who he exchanged remarks about the girl with the large breasts, who also sat at the table, where they handled fossils, crystals, and geodes.

This guy was not a friend, just a classmate, who said, Matt remembered, his father was wounded at Omaha Beach in World War II, losing his eyesight.

Matt recalled telling the guy, that after graduating at the end of the term, he was going to travel to Spain, and try to do fiction writing. The geology class was one of the last classes Matt had to take for completing the requirements for his Bachelor's degree.

Weeks after graduating, while preparing for the trip to Spain, Matt remembered this guy from geology class phoned and asked if he was really going to Spain.

It was a shock getting that phone call; Matt was upset, he remembered, feeling he was being informed on.

It was just part of the puzzle of why he was being watched in the first place.

"Hey," Matt said looking out the car window, "you can see out over the desert for miles—look at that."

The car was level now, as they drove across the dusty plaza.

CHAPTER 13

Outside the car, Matt stood watching Doris and the two girls walking toward the souvenir shop next to the cathedral.

There were few other tourists in the plaza, which added to the feeling of desolation for Matt as he looked off at the horizon.

Then the pain in his stomach came back, sharper now, and he put his hand on the spot and leaned back on the Thunderbird fender.

Alex saw Matt was in pain, and said, "We should have stopped for something to eat." He was putting clip-on sunshades over the lenses of his eyeglasses. When he put the glasses back on, he looked up at the sky, testing for brightness.

"I need a—drink," Matt said, slow, sitting up, but still on the fender. "My guts hurt bad."

"Doris keeps some Crème de Menth in the glove box," Alex said grinning. "She keeps a bottle of it for travel-food—that upsets her stomach. There might be some."

Matt moved quickly to sit in the front passenger seat, then pulled open the glove box door.

He searched through maps and combs, and pushing away paper napkins and a hairbrush, found the half-pint bottle with a faded label.

"This is a lifesaver," Matt said holding up the flat bottle to check the amount.

"Don't look like much is left," Alex said, "maybe a quarter of it."

"It'll work—no matter," Matt said before he drank all the green liquid, holding the bottle up to get every drop.

Grinning, Alex looked away and saw Doris and the girls with a young woman wearing a red jacket, who was standing in the doorway of the store.

"Looks like the girls found a tour guide over there," Alex said. "We better go join them."

"That green stuff helped," Matt said as they were walking. "It took that burn away."

Matt looked off in the distance as he was walking, past the edge of the dirt plaza, where the country spread out all the way to the horizon. In places, miles away, there were more stone towers rising above the tan desert. And in some places, the sun came through a break in the clouds, and shined like a spotlight on patches of ground.

"You know Alex," Matt said in a kidding tone, "I think I can see the Gulf of Mexico—over there—off in the distance."

"The Conquistadores came from that direction," Alex said, "looking for gold."

Matt shaded his eyes, as if it would help see further in the distance, "I think the Indians here—could see the Spaniards coming—they could see them coming for days."

"Yeah," Alex said, "and they knew it meant trouble. They had heard from other tribes about the Spanish. They wanted gold—they were looking for the Seven Cities of Gold—El Dorado—and they came with a vengeance."

Doris and the girls were standing at the cathedral door with the girls in the red jacket; when they all went inside, Matt and Alex turned away, and walked to look down below from the edge of the plaza.

"This place would be easy to defend," Matt said looking at the steep drop off.

"There was a hell of a battle here," Alex said peering over the edge cautiously. "I read about it. The Indians held them off. The Spaniards couldn't get up here—it went on six or seven days."

Doris and the girls came out of the cathedral with the girl in the red jacket, and walked over to Alex and Matt.

"They made a movie in that church," the youngest girl said. "What do you think of that?"

"What's the name of the movie?" Matt asked her.

"Something like 'Death Comes To The Cathedral' I think," she said. "A woman wrote the book they made into the movie."

The girl in the red jacket, said quietly, "It was 'Death Comes To The Archbishop.'" She was an Indian with a narrow face.

"I'll look it up in the library," Matt said. Then looking out at the desert again, he asked, "Are there any other Indian pueblos—up on the top of outcroppings—like this one?"

"No," the girl said looking at him. "Acoma is the only reservation like this."

"The Spanish," Alex said to the girl, "what did they do when they couldn't get up here? What did they do?"

"The fighting went on," she said looking out at the desert, "until they found a way up. They did—finally get up here. A traitor showed them a secret way up."

Alex shook his head, saying, "There's always one."

"They could have lasted forever," Matt said, "if they had enough food and water up here—you'd think."

"There's water in a place over there," the thin girl said pointing. "It's a deep pool in the rock that fills with rain water. It's never empty."

"It's windy up here," Alex's youngest daughter said, folding her arms. "I'm getting cold."

"C'mon girls," Doris said pulling the oldest girl by the arm, "we'll go back to the car."

Everyone was walking toward the car parked by the store, when Matt asked, "Do they sell beer at the store there?"

"No," the girl said walking, but not looking at him "There's no selling alcohol on Indian Reservations."

"That figures," Matt said. Then he turned to take a look out at the horizon again.

"It's really something to see," Alex said, looking at Matt as they were walking. "You can't describe this place—you have to see it for yourself."

"Yeah," Matt said nodding, "the view makes you forget—even a hangover. I've never seen anything like this—it's like a different world up here. It's worth a trip here—even on a Sunday morning."

Alex grinned, moving his eyeglasses up higher on his nose, a finger and thumb reaching to hold the edges of the lenses.

"I told you," he said, "the trip was worth it."

The clouds overhead were getting darker, as they drove back down the road from the rocky tower, the road where bulldozers were working to make the level less steep.

At the highway, Alex turned west, instead of east, the direction back to Albuquerque.

"Hey," Matt said, "I thought we were heading home."

"I want to buy some—items," Alex said. "There's a store over in Grants that sells Zuni Indian stuff. It won't take long."

"He buys those Indian Konica dolls," Doris said while lighting a cigarette with the car lighter from inside the glove box door. "We got a dozen dolls lined up on a shelf in the girl's bedroom," she said putting the lighter back in its holder. It was then she saw the empty Crème de Menth bottle, and held it up.

"Yeah," Alex said looking at her for a moment. "I gave it to Matt for his hangover. I'll fill it, back at the bar," he added, and Doris said nothing, just put the flat bottle back in the glove box.

"I'm getting hungry," the younger girl said. "Can we stop for a burger?"

"I want fries—and ketchup," the older girl said.

"They have a cafeteria at the trading post," Alex said, turning his head to the girls for a second. "We can eat there—it's just over the border in Arizona. Hold on a bit."

"Look," Doris said, "the sign says Gallup is that way—just like in the song, 'Route Sixty-Six.'"

"That's an odd name," the older girl said. "Even out here in the desert."

"There's another name, 'Truth Or Consequences' for a town out here in New Mexico," Doris said, "but I don't know where it is—exactly. It was named after a radio quiz program."

"I want ketchup and fries too," the younger girl said.

At the table in the cafeteria of the trading post, Matt was sitting opposite the women, while Alex was over at the counter, selecting Konica dolls.

They were all eating hamburgers, when the youngest girl said, "He's crying—look Matt's crying."

Matt's throat had grown tight, suddenly. He could not swallow. It was as if a hand was gripping his throat, and a sinking feeling overwhelmed him that he could not stop.

His emotions were pulling him down, and he felt powerless to stop it; it seemed a hand inside his chest was pulling at his insides.

He lot out a sob, almost choking to stop another one from coming. Then he lowered his head to hide his face.

"Alex," Doris called across to her husband. "Alex come!"

Leaving the display of Indian dolls, Alex quickly walked to the table and stood behind Matt, who was convulsing, tears running down his cheeks.

"What's the matter, fella?" he asked, taking the half-eaten hamburger out of his hand.

"I can't—stop it," Matt said and stopped to take in air, his head down. "I don't know—what it is."

"Is he sick?" Doris asked in a protective tone, looking at her two daughters. "What's the matter with him, Alex?" she said looking up at her husband. "Can you do something—or should I call—for help?"

"Why is he crying" the youngest girl asked in a tone that was compassionate, and at the same time inquisitive.

"He's having a—breakdown," Alex said quietly. "An emotional breakdown."

"But why is he crying?" she asked again.

"Because he's sad," Alex said looking at Matt who sat almost doubled over. "He's feeling—very sad. And he can't stop it."

"Alex, do something," Doris said, "people are looking."

"Okay," Alex said to her, quietly. Then lifting Matt up by his underarms from the chair, added, "C'mon fella, we'll go out to the car." He looked at Doris and she nodded.

When he had Matt standing, Alex pushed the chair away with his foot.

Outside at the car, after Matt sat down in the front seat, Alex, leaning on the open door, said, "Maybe you should see a doctor, Matt—I mean while we're here in Albuquerque."

"I haven't got any money," Matt answered not looking up.

"You were in the army," Alex said. "There's a Veteran's hospital here—you can go there. They'll look at you—help you out. Maybe prescribe some kind of pills—to help you get over this and make you feel better."

Matt drew a deep breath, but it turned into a choking sob.

"I—don't care," he said breathing shallow. "I just want it to stop."

"I know," Alex said, turning his head to look at the trading post. "We'll get you to a doctor—get you some help." Then he added, "Here come the girls—they're shook up."

"Sorry for getting sick," Matt said. "Sorry it happened out here—on a road trip. But I can't help it."

"It's just your nerves," Alex said. "They can only take so much—then they snap."

"Sorry for upsetting your girls," Matt said.

"They don't understand—that's all," Alex said as the girls approached the car. He opened the back door for them.

The three of them climbed into the back car seat, the younger one in the middle. They were silent.

Matt could see on their faces that they were wondering if he was going to get violent. They were all afraid.

"This never happened to me before," he said.

★ ★ ★

After filling out the forms at the Veterans Administration Hospital, Matt was shown into the doctor's office.

The office was in a room off the lobby, and when Matt entered, he saw the doctor sitting at a desk, reading his application closely.

He was a young man with sandy hair, wearing a white coat over a green hospital uniform.

"The psychological staff won't be back until Monday morning," the doctor said looking up at Matt. "You will have to come back then. I would help if I could—but this is not my area—my specialty in medicine."

When Matt stepped out of the office, he saw the doctor go back to reading the application.

Alex was standing in the lobby.

"You going to be admitted?" he asked.

"I got to wait until Monday morning," Matt said, "to see the doctors in the mental health department." He could feel the tears coming to his eyes again. "They're the only ones who can admit me."

"You want to stay in Albuquerque?" Alex asked.

"Yeah—I think I should."

"You can get a motel room" Alex said, "and Monday morning come back—for treatment."

"I guess that's the way I'll have to go," Matt said.

"I'll put the motel bill on my charge card," Alex said as they were walking out of the lobby. "You got any money to eat on?"

"Yeah," Matt said.

Alex grinned, knowing he was being lied to.

At the car, the two men climbed in front, as Doris asked, "You coming back to Taos, Matt?" from the back seat.

"He's staying until Monday morning," Alex said to her. "He's going to get a motel room tonight—and go back to the hospital tomorrow morning."

"Okay," Doris said. "The girls are tired—they want to get home."

CHAPTER 14

It was almost nine o'clock the next morning, when Matt woke up in the motel room. He lay thinking for a moment, looking at the crack in the light panel above the bed.

The heavy wave of emotion that pulled him down, was now gone. It was as if a drug passed through him; and was spent.

"Damn," he said scratching the hair stubble on his chin, "this place is dumpy. I got to get away from here—and I got to get away from that Veteran's hospital too."

Swinging his feet to the floor, he sat hesitating to get up, looking at the bright sunlight on the floor, coming through the blinds on the window.

"How the hell am I going to get back to Taos?" he said pulling off his t-shirt over his head. "I'll have to hitch-hike—I'm flat broke."

Looking at his crumpled pants on the floor, an idea came to him.

"Alex paid for two nights at this motel," he said rubbing his chin, "and I can get a refund—if I leave before eleven. I can use the refund to buy a bus ticket—bingo."

After a long, hot shower, he put on his ski jacket, and went out to the office to claim the money.

At the Trailways Bus station, he asked the clerk for a ticket to Taos. He was a dollar thirty-five short.

The clerk said, "Buy a ticket for the money you got. You can hitch-hike the rest of the way—to Taos."

"Okay," Matt said through the barred window, "I'll do that," and slid the money into the opening.

"This ticket will take you to—Pillar—a town about twelve miles south of Taos," the clerk said.

"I never thought of doing it this way," Matt said putting the ticket in his jacket pocket. "Hey, what time does the bus leave?"

"Two o'clock sharp."

Over at the bench in the lobby, Matt sat down, then took out the blue ticket to look at it.

"Ask the driver to let you stay on the bus to Taos," an even low voice said.

Matt looked at the wide-faced Indian next to him. He had a brush haircut, and wore a new Levi jacket and pants.

"I heard you say Taos," the Indian said, "but you're short of money. The driver will let you ride—you ask him."

"Okay," Matt said nodding.

When the loudspeaker announced the bus leaving for Arizona, the Indian stood up, taking a crumpled paper bag off the seat next to him.

"Thanks for the tip—about the driver," Matt said to the Indian before he walked away. Then under his breath, added, "I hope it works. Damn—damn—I hate being broke. All the time—I'm broke."

He sat thinking, looking around the crowded bus station, asking himself why he found himself sitting here today, far away from his plan to do fiction writing. He was looking for an explanation of how his emotions could plunge to such depths. He was looking for the reason that caused the crying in such a desperate reaction.

Then he caught himself asking if it came from <u>outside</u> himself—if someone used drugs, or maybe some kind of electric shock. "Who would do that?" he asked himself.

"I've got to stop thinking that kind of stuff," he whispered, then stood up.

Walking, putting his hands in his pockets, he came to the large window at the front of the bus station, and looked out at the street outside.

Cars were passing on the wide main street outside, glinting in the sunlight. There were tall buildings and sidewalks like any other city. It was hard for him to realize Albuquerque was out in the New Mexico desert, sand in every direction just beyond the city limits.

Looking up at the clock in the bus station lobby, he saw he had over two hours before his bus would leave.

He shrugged, then walked outside looking for some kind of distraction to pass the time.

He did not want to dwell anymore on what caused the burst of emotion that caused the rollercoaster into the depths that made him cry.

It had never happened before, and he felt it was not a part of him. But it did frighten him.

The bus station was on a street corner, and when Matt crossed the street, he came up to a large church front.

A panel sign outside a low building next to the church read: FREE DINNER 1PM—ALL WELCOME.

A line of people was standing near the stairway that lead up to the door of the low building.

Matt smiled, thinking it was free, and what did he have to lose. He had not thought about food; he was not accustomed to eating regular.

Stepping to the end of the line, he looked at the people standing ahead of him. The guy in front of him wore a full-face beard, and stood, hands in pickets, rocking from side to side.

"What do they give you for dinner?" Matt asked the beard. "Spaghetti? Beans and hot dogs?"

The bearded man, looking straight ahead, said slow, "A—vegetable soup, two pieces of white bread, a dry donut, and a cup of coffee."

"That's some menu," Matt said.

"It's all the old stuff," the bearded man said continuing to stare forward, while rocking sideways, "that restaurants throw out."

When the metal door opened at the top of the stairs, Matt saw a monk appear dressed in a white robe with a rope tied around his waist.

The first one up the steps was a woman with white hair, and she began talking loud to the monk, who nodded as she passed. She had no teeth.

"I'm Doris Day," Matt heard her say. "I like it here—that's why I come."

Matt sat down at a long table. Across from him were two young men that looked like runaways. One wore glasses that had a white tape, or band-aid, holding the eyeglass frame together at the temple.

A banner on the wall read: SAINT FRANCIS XAVIER PARISH HALL.

When Matt saw the people at the end of the room, passing an opening in the wall, where another monk was handing out bowls of food, he realized it was a self-serve cafeteria.

The place settings before each chair, where there were bread, donuts, a coffee mug and silverware, had Matt thinking he would be served at the table.

He grinned about the table service, as he stood up from the table to get in line for a bowl of soup.

When Matt brought the bowl back to the table, he sat looking at the pink mixture; it had possibly started out as tomato soup, but when the other vegetables were added, it changed color. He saw green beans and cauliflower in the mix.

When he tasted the soup, Matt made a face; the soup was sour, and he put the spoon down.

He was eating the dry donut, dunking it in the coffee, when he saw the monk at the wall opening, watching him. The monk was a young man with a fleshy face. Matt was sure he did not eat the soup he was serving.

Just then, a grey haired Negro man in overalls, who had been sitting at the end of the table, slumped off his chair, and lay on his side on the floor.

The cook, a bald man in white apron, came out of the kitchen, and knelt down, feeling the Negro's wrist for pulse.

"Better call an ambulance," he said back to the young Monk watching through the serving opening in the wall.

At the same time, Matt saw a man wearing an old army coat, who was sitting next to the Negro's chair, reach over to take the slices of bread and donut from the Negro's place setting, and slip them in his pocket.

"I think I've hit bottom," Matt said to himself. "I can't get no lower—than all this. All I wanted to be—was a writer: look where I ended up."

He stood up and, walking to the door, saw by the wall clock he had about a half-hour before his bus departed for Taos.

"I should have never come here," he said walking down the steps. "I'm not one of these people—I don't belong here. I belong writing stores."

* * *

Riding on the bus that splashed through melting snow water on the highway, Matt sat watching the shadows on the mountains growing longer with the sun going down.

He felt embarrassed going back to Taos where people knew him. He felt a mild anger about not getting any help at the hospital in Albuquerque. And most of all, he was puzzled, trying to understand how his emotions could drop so low, that he was reduced to crying.

This was all new to him; it made him suspicious now.

He even had thoughts that the depression that came over him was induced, somehow, by someone.

Darkness closed in after the bus stopped in Santa Fe, taking on four more passengers. As the ride toward Taos grew shorter, his ticket only good to Pillar, he felt uneasy about asking the driver to let him stay on the bus to Taos.

There it was again, he thought. Being broke was forcing him to beg, ask the driver to let him ride free the twelve miles from Pillar to Taos. It was always that way, he thought; he was always begging from someone.

It seemed that a writer has to become a mooch, he thought, in order to get time to do his writing.

Matt shifted in the seat, looking forward in the dark bus, except for a few lights scattered on the overhead, where passengers were reading in their seats, below. He stood up, forcing himself to walk forward between the seats.

It was either ask the driver, he thought, or you had to hitch-hike, or even walk, the damn twelve miles. And it was dark now.

"My ticket only goes to Pillar," Matt said to the driver, whose face was lighted by the glow of small lights on the dashboard, "but I live in Taos. Can I ride to Taos? My money ran out."

Matt held the ticket in one hand, while he held onto the pole behind the driver's seat with the other.

The driver, looking forward at the road, said, "Give me the ticket when you get off in Taos."

"Right," Matt said, wanting to thank him, but caught himself, thinking it was better to keep quiet. He smiled.

Later, when the bus was passing through the dark town of Pillar, without stopping, Matt felt relieved. He had cleared the hurdle of asking the driver, and now he was riding, not walking or hitchhiking, and it made him feel better about himself and his abilities.

When the bus stopped in Taos, Matt made sure he was the last passenger in line going up the aisle to the door.

"Thanks," he said handing the driver the ticket, then stepped down and off the bus.

The driver was silent as he closed the door.

Matt saw the bus had stopped at the corner of the Taos Plaza, where, across the highway, was the alleyway that lead to Marci's Ufer house.

"Maybe she has something to drink," Matt said crossing the highway in a quick-step. "I've got a good excuse for missing her paint-party last night. Wait until I tell her about all the things that happened in Albuquerque—that'll get me off the hook."

CHAPTER 15

All the lights were on inside Marci's house, but the front door was locked.
Matt, grinning, tapped on the window with the new putty, that was giving her a sense of security, and he thought that was funny.

"Hey, Matt," Marci said opening the door. "You break out of that hospital—in Albuquerque?"

"I never even got in," he said unzipping his jacket.

"That's what I thought," she said, her voice dropping to a deep roll, "when I heard all that—about you having a crack-up. I didn't believe <u>any</u> of that—the rumors."

Her voice made him feel comfortable, and he followed her, smiling, into the kitchen.

The teenager, Margaret, wearing an apron was leaning over a cookie sheet on the end of the table. The baby, in the wicker basket, rested at the other end of the table.

"What you making?" Matt said to Margaret, taking off his jacket, dropping it over the back of a chair.

"Valentine cookies," Margaret said looking up. "I'm taking them to school tomorrow for the kids—for everyone."

Matt watched as Marci and her daughter sprinkled red sugar on the heart-shaped cookies in the flat tin tray, then slide the tray into the oven of the narrow stove.

"Tomorrow's Valentine Day," Margaret said, noticing how Matt was looking at Marci, and pulled her sweater down tight over her pointed breasts, but did not look at him.

"What kind of cookies are they?" Matt said, pretending to care.

"They're just sugar-cookies," Marci answered while wiping her hands in a dishtowel. "We made four dozen. Try one."

"No thanks," Matt said, beginning to feel like an intruder in this family project. He was looking for a place to sit down, and at the same time, thinking about asking for a drink.

There was no place to sit in the small kitchen.

"I heard all about Albuquerque," Marci said, "when I ran into Alex on my way home from the super market. He told me all about—leaving you at the Veterans Hospital."

"Yeah," Matt said, "they said I might be a chronic—drinker, but they don't admit people to the psycho-ward for that."

"How did you get back?" Marci asked putting a mixing bowl and spoons in the sink, then reaching over to put the cookie cutters in too. She caught Matt watching her, and smiled.

"By bus," he said smiling back. "I just got back—got off the bus—so I came over here. I'll be heading for my apartment—in a while—I got things I have to—"

"What's your hurry?" Marci said bumping Matt with her hip.

A timer went off, and Margaret went to the oven and slid the cookie tray out.

"This is the last batch," Marci said to Margaret, who was scooping the hot cookies up with a spatula, setting them on a wire rack to cool, "and it's time for a break."

"You got any beer?" Matt asked Marci. "Something, maybe left over from the party?"

"Oh yeah," she said. "Vodka and half a bottle of scotch, but—maybe you—better stick to beer—for a while."

"I'm going up to take a bath," Margaret said interrupting, taking off her apron. She noticed her mother and Matt eyeing one another, and wanted to leave them alone. "I'll put the cookies in the tin box tomorrow—before I go to school."

"Okay, honey," Marci said. "Matt and me want to talk a while—"

"Nancy's sleeping like a log," Margaret said looking down at the baby in the wicker basket, while hanging a hot pad glove on its wall hook at the same time. "I'll take her upstairs—to my bedroom."

"I'll check on you later," Marci said to her. "Matt and I want to talk—for a while."

Margaret knew what was going on; she knew they wanted one another. She picked up the baby basket by the handle and walked out of the kitchen without speaking.

"I'll get you a beer," Marci said to Matt, touching his face with her fingers.

"Oh, yeah," he said, when she handed him a bottle from the refrigerator. "This is my first drink—in two days."

"Come sit in the studio," Marci said watching him open the bottle and sip a drink.

He followed her into the dim light coming through the overhead skylight, and he saw most of the squares on the big wall canvas were mostly all filled—painted with all types of logos.

The boards creaked overhead with Margaret walking up there in her room.

"Quick," Marci whispered, "take your pants off—we'll get under the covers on the bed. We got to talk."

He set the beer on the floor, watching her pull off her light sweater over her head.

Matt felt the full length of her in the bed, she lying on her side against him under the covers.

"Elliott and me," she whispered to the side of Matt's face, "we're—finished. He can't leave his wife—her lawyers got him fixed to lose everything—the house, alimony—child support."

"Can she do that?" Matt whispered back. "Get all that?"

"Yeah, they're claiming—desertion—or something—and her lawyer is cleaning him out of everything."

"That's a hell of a price—for your freedom," Matt said, moving his hand to her hip, sliding it up and down. "I said that might happen—but I was just trying to be a wise guy."

"He'll be free," she said putting her hand on his groin, "but he'll be broke. He'll come to Taos—broke—flat broke."

"Is that what he wants to do?"

"Yeah," Marci said rolling her stomach against his, "but I don't want him to."

"What does that mean?"

"I got two kids—to take care of," Marci said, her breathing growing quicker. "I need—security."

"Everybody needs security, Marci."

"Let's—do it," she whispered. "C'mon, let's do it now."

"You don't want to get pregnant—again—" he said. "I hope you don't."

"The doctor fixed me inside," she whispered, pulling him on top of her. "He wants my—insides—to—rest."

Matt was up on his elbows over her, moving the blanket to cover himself.

When he was in her wetness, she whispered, "Get working—C'mon—C'mon."

Matt was in a frenzy, but he held off the climax.

"Hold—hold—oh, man—hold," Marci said pulling him against herself.

Finally, he could hold the climax no longer, and let go.

"Oh, oh-h," she said as Matt slid off her wet body. "That was—lovely—that was—nice—we should get married."

Matt was lying next to her again.

"You said that," he said quietly, "the last time, too."

"It's all different now," she said still breathing in short pauses. "We could really—get married—with a license. I'm—not just talking—about the sex part."

"Oh, I see," He said, rolling the opposite way to pick up the beer bottle he set on the floor.

He was taking a drink, when Marci said in a deep whisper, "You could get a steady job—on a newspaper—and we could make a life together."

He was thinking now, it was not a good idea to come here to Marci's, after getting off the bus.

"I have to hold off getting married," Matt said slowly, wanting to set her down gently, yet not lose her, "until—well, I came to Taos to write my book."

Rolling against his side again, she whispered, "You can't be a bar swamper—the rest of your life, Matt. You'll eventually—have to settle down."

"Yeah, I know," he said, and took a long drink of beer, "and I have to tell you—I went through all this stuff before—when I got out of the university. My girl wanted me to settle down too—get married and all that. So—she married somebody else."

"And—we were—really crazy about one another," he added in a whisper for himself to hear.

He envisioned a flash of a sunny fall afternoon, the trees bright with yellow color, him walking on campus with her, Deirdre, her wealth showing in her long blond-streaked hair, Tartan skirt and cashmere sweater.

He looked up at the dark skylight.

"Matt, honey, that is all in the past."

"She came from a wealthy family," he said as if he had not heard Marci, "and her father wanted her to marry somebody who would keep her living—comfortably—like she was accustomed to."

"Matt," Marci said pressing against him under the blanket, "you can still work on your book. You just have to get a job—that is steady—with an income."

"Nah," he said thinking of what brought him to Taos, "that wouldn't be the same, Marci. I want to be a full-time scribbler—that's all I want to do."

"What's the name," Marci said in a tone that was heavy with her calculating to break down Matt's plans, "of this book you are writing?"

"I call it, 'The Carrot, The String, and The Stick,'" he said. "But that could change—it's just a working title for my first draft—of the manuscript."

"What's the book about, Matt? What's the story about?"

"It's about—a guy writing a book," he said feeling defensive, "and what it costs him—in terms of what he loses from life. He's like the donkey in the parable that goes for the carrot dangled out in front of him—which is—the book—the book is the carrot out front of him."

"It's hard to understand, Matt, but it seems there's no room—in this writer's life—for anybody else."

"You're right," Matt said while quietly thinking. "And there's a new problem creeping in—booze is catchin-up on the writer."

"Which means," she said, the challenge in her voice less forceful, "what is happening with you and alcohol."

"I don't know how it's going to work out, Marci. I'm being honest—with you—and myself." Reaching for the beer bottle, he found it empty. "I might wind up in some kind of alcohol treatment at a hospital."

"I would be willing to help," Marci said. "No matter how bad it got."

Setting the bottle back on the floor, Matt said, "I had this feeling when I was at a church cafeteria for a free meal down in Albuquerque—that I was sinking in life. That I was becoming a bum—a down-and-outer—and I didn't like it."

"Yeah, Matt—that is scary."

He felt her move, to get comfortable, while she was still leaning against him.

"I just came here to do the writing on the "Carrot" book," he said, sensing he had said too much now; he felt self-conscious about spilling his problems out any more. "I got blindsided—by booze—that's all."

"Where do you go from here, Matt? What you going to do?"

"There's only <u>one</u> thing, I can do," he said feeling her skin turning hot again. "I'll just keep writing—until I can't anymore."

"You'll be all right, honey," Marci said rubbing his stomach. "Don't worry—don't think so much."

"Maybe you're right," he said turning on his side to face her.

When they made love, Marci held nothing back, and Matt sensed desperation in her frenzy.

As much as he and Marci made love—he never felt about her in the way he felt about Deirdre. He had always wanted to be with Deirdre—spend as much time as he could with her.

He had never felt that way before Deirdre, and with all the girls that came after, he never felt it again.

Later, Marci dropped off in a deep sleep, breathing heavy in an even manner, and Matt lay thinking how he needed her, and at the same time, wanted to leave.

The sound of a quick rapping came from the front door.

"Marci?" a man's voice in a harsh whisper called. "Hey, Marci."

Matt shook her until she opened her eyes.

"There's someone at the front door," he whispered, resting his hand over her mouth.

"It can't be Elliott," she whispered back, holding his hand away.

"I don't recognize the voice."

"Come <u>with</u> me," she said pushing him off the edge of the bed with both hands, then pulling the blanket to wrap around herself.

Matt followed her to the door, lifting some of her blanket around himself.

"Who is it?" Marci said, her ear to the door.

"Pablo."

"Just a second," Marci said, then after looking at Matt and shrugging, unlocked the door, opening it to the length of the short chain just in front of her face.

"Here's your two joints," Pablo said in an even whisper, "like I said I'd give you."

Marci took them through the narrow door opening.

"Okay. Thanks, Pablo."

"I'm going to use the fuel tank room," Pablo said in a total whisper, "later—later tonight."

"We got to be—careful," Marci whispered, holding the two cigarettes in one hand, the blanket in the other, both up, covering her face. "Is it really—I mean is it a must—that you come here—use the room?

There was a pause.

"My mother wants me to come home—see her."

Marci puffed her cheeks and turned to Matt.

He shrugged, as if saying the decision was hers.

"All right, Pablo," Marci said, her voice forced raspy. "But we got to use our heads—I don't want the cops crashing in here. You should only use it to hide—once in a while."

"I'm careful, Marci."

"I'm—counting on you. I got to think of my two girls," Marci said like a schoolteacher. "I'm going to close the door." When she was locking the door, she whispered to Matt, "I wish he would leave Taos."

"He's asking for it," Matt said quietly when he and Marci were back in bed under the blanket. Stretching out on the bed, full-length, he could sense her worrying; her body was tight.

To reassure her, he said, "Pablo keeps sneaking around town, like he's doing—someone's bound to spot him."

Marci put her arm across Matt's chest.

"You should move in here," she said in a rasping whisper.

CHAPTER 16

Tuesday morning, Matt was telling Alex what happened in Albuquerque at the hospital before his bus ride back to Taos, while they worked cleaning the bar.

Monk, who worked Sunday during the "mystery trip," had not cleaned the bar, and Alex did not either on Monday, and the place smelled like an ashtray.

Matt had finished vacuuming the front rugs, and was mopping the back poolroom, when Phillip Dent came through the front door that had been open to let fresh air circulate inside. Matt, wringing out the mop in the hall, saw Dent sit down on a stool up by the window, and begin talking to Alex, quietly, over the bar.

Walking to the front of the bar to close the door, when the mopping was done, Matt heard Dent say to Alex, "I had to put her in the mental hospital—she's turned worse lately."

Everybody in Taos was sorry for Dent's wife; she was young, and good looking, but mentally sick.

Matt shook his head, not wanting to hear more.

After closing the front door, Matt took the one beer he was allotted for his cleaning work, and sat at the far end of the bar so he would not hear Alex and Dent talking.

He did not want to intrude.

When he finished his beer, he dropped the empty in the tub, then going to the door, said "I'm going home to clean up, change clothes."

Alex just nodded in understanding, and Matt could see the concern on his face as he listened to Phillip. It was the same concern that had helped him in Albuquerque, and he felt grateful there were people like Alex.

Outside, the bright sun was making the daytime warmer now, he thought, but the nights were still cold. He grinned.

Cold nights reminded him of Marci, and her bed in the studio, and he said to himself, when stepping off the end of the plaza sidewalk, "I'm not going to move in with her. I want to stay free—and I don't need her problems, either."

* * *

Back at his apartment, Matt was shaving, when he heard the firm knocking at the door. "Who—is it?" he shouted.

"Your landlord," Mister Romero shouted back.

"Okay," Matt said walking to the door, shaving cream still on half his face. "Coming."

Pulling open the door, he said quickly, "I know I'm late with the rent—but I just need a couple more days, and I will—"

Mister Romero stood nodding, looking at Matt through his glasses with heavy black plastic frames.

"Let me talk to you," Mister Romero said, as he stepped inside. He was much shorter than Matt, but had wide shoulders.

Matt watched him come in the apartment and look at the pile of typing papers on the table. Then, after looking at the pile of Life magazines on the floor, under the table, sat down in a kitchen chair.

Mister Romero was president of the town council, and looked every inch, in the white shirts he always wore, very capable of handling the job.

"I know you do writing," Mister Romero said to Matt, who now, sat down in the chair at the opposite end of the table, "and I know you work at that cantina in town—and you don't make much money."

"Yes," Matt said, "but I'm planning to sell my type-writer—and with the money—pay—"

Mister Romero reached over and opened the door of the small refrigerator under the sink.

Matt could see the half-pack of dried out cheese slices on the shelf inside, next to an empty mustard jar. There was an empty peanut butter jar on the shelf below, and behind it, an empty cardboard box labeled Ginger Snaps.

"Could you paint an apartment?" Mister Romero asked, when closing the refrigerator door.

"Sure," Matt said, feeling suddenly relieved of paying the rent money. "This one?"

"No—number four—down on the end," Mister Romero said looking at the typewriter on the table. "The old lady—Miss Harker—moved back to Lubbock, Texas. She was a painter, who liked to paint white birch trees with yellow leaves, all the time. Her apartment is vacant now—and I want to paint it before I rent it again."

"Sure, I'll paint it," Matt said.

"That will cover this month's rent," Mister Romero said slowly, "and that's all you get."

"Okay," Matt said, feeling a smile coming but keeping a straight face. "Do you have the paint?"

"Yes. All you need is in the room already."

"I'll start tomorrow," Matt said, nodding.

When Mister Romero stood up, he was all chest, that exuded authority, and Matt remembered, once when they were talking about the town council, he said the people trusted him, and "they vote the way I tell them."

* * *

The next morning, Matt worked steadily to clean the bar, after telling Alex about the paint job on the apartment, and was in a hurry to get started.

"I'll take my beer ration with me today," Matt said. "The sooner I get started, the sooner I'll get done."

Alex stood wiping a bar glass, turning it on a towel, and looking out the front window, while Matt checked under the hard boiled egg basket and found four quarters and slipped them into his pocket. There were five eggs left in the basket, and he nodded, remembering the amount.

"Hey," Alex said, "looking across the plaza—ain't that guy standing in front of the Sheriff's office—the guy in the tan raincoat—ain't he the same guy that was at Acoma?"

Matt, straightened up from taking his free can of beer from the cooler, looked to the other side of the town plaza, squinting.

"He looks like Peter Lorre," Matt said. "The movie actor."

"Right," Alex said looking over the top of his eye-glasses to see clearer, "I'm sure—I saw him at Acoma last Sunday—he was over by the cathedral—when we were up there."

"Maybe he's with the movie crowd," Matt said, walking down the bar to turn the corner, out. "I hear they're back in town."

"Could be," Alex said, setting the glass in his hand with the stack already on the back bar. "Some of the work crew came in for a drink—last night."

"Has that Hopper guy come back in?" Matt asked as he pulled open the front door.

"No—just those technicians were in for a drink," Alex said looking out the front window again. "And I haven't seen Peter Fonda either."

*   *   *

It had started raining, and later turned to a drizzle, Matt saw out the apartment open door, as he was painting the shelves in a cubbyhole with the light blue paint.

The door was left open to carry away paint fumes.

He worked with a lamp on the floor next to him, the shade off, for a light to see skipped places he missed with the brush. For a stool, he used one of the gallon paint cans that was full.

After he worked more than an hour, steadily, the paint fumes grew too strong. He turned away from the cubbyhole and set the brush on the edge of the paint can.

Stretching his back by sitting up straight, he looked out the open door.

A pick-up truck, spattered with mud, was moving around the corner of an adobe house over in the barrio, behind the wall at the back of the Romero property. The truck had a horse trailer in tow with a sticker on the side: VISIT EL PASO.

When the truck stopped next to the well, Matt reached down and snapped off the lamp on the floor, while still watching.

The driver stepped out, a man in a cowboy hat, the rim rolled on both sides, and wearing a faded western Levi jacket.

Pablo climbed out of the passenger door, covering his head and shoulder with a green blanket; Matt nudged the door partly closed with his toe, continuing to watch.

From where he sat, Matt could see the horse trailer was parked to block any view of the men's actions from the houses in the barrio.

Pablo bent down into the well, hanging over the edge for a few moments, then came up with two long bundles wrapped in black trash bags.

The guy in the cowboy hat followed Pablo, when he went back to the truck passenger seat, where he unwrapped the two packages, rifles, out of the light rain.

The guy in the cowboy hat looked at the two rifles closely, from one end to the other, and nodded.

While Pablo sat re-wrapping the rifles, Matt watched as the cowboy hat walked back to the muddy trailer, and reaching under where the hitch connected to the trailer, came up with a package the size of a carton of cigarettes.

"Well," Matt said to himself, "that concludes that drug deal." Smiling, he added, "And Pablo gets to keep the rifles with the telescopic sights—they're worth a lot more."

Matt sat waiting until the truck disappeared back around the corner of the house, before he turned the light back on, continuing his painting.

*　　*　　*

Next morning, while they were cleaning the bar, Alex told Matt about Marci leaving last night from the bar with a guy from the Sheriff's Office—the town womanizer.

"I think she's looking for a guy with a steady income," Matt said grinning. "That leaves me out—I can't even make enough money to keep me above water."

"You spend enough time over at her house," Alex said. "I'm surprised you haven't moved in over there."

"Yeah," Matt said wiping out the ashtrays with a wet cloth, "she asked me to move in—get a steady job and all that."

"You know," Alex said spraying the back bar mirror, then wiping it, "she's been married twice—and nobody knows who the father of that baby she has is."

Matt shrugged, then went back to the storeroom and brought out a case of Budweiser.

"How's the book going?" Alex said spraying the part of the mirror over the cash register. "You making any progress?"

"Slow but sure," Matt said, feeling surprised at Alex's question. "When I'm painting—I got a lot of time to think about the book story-line."

Matt was stacking the beer bottles in the cooler.

"You know," he said reaching for more bottles, "I got a short story making the rounds to magazines." He said it as if he had just remembered.

"I see," Alex said wiping the mirror, "when you sell a story to a magazine,—you got money to work on the book—if the story sells."

"Yeah," Matt said reaching for more bottles, "that was my plan—but the cost of postage put me in the poor house. And here I am—working here."

When the cardboard case on the floor was empty of bottles, Matt took it down the bar to the storeroom.

When he came back, and was reaching in the cooler for his one daily beer, Alex said, "Good luck with the painting—that shouldn't take too long to finish."

"You know," Matt said going to the door, "I almost forgot about that story I sent out. I'm going by the Post Office now, see if I got an answer from the editor."

"By the way," Alex said, "two eggs were sold last night."

"I'll get the quarters tomorrow," Matt said going out the door.

At the Post Office, the clerk handed Matt a large envelope, and he winced.

His short story was returned from the magazine editor in the self addressed stamped envelope, the crease in the middle, showing where he had folded it in half, to put it in the first envelope along with the typed pages of the story.

He did not open the envelope; just carried it as he walked by one corner.

As he walked on the road to the Romero house, he had the same feeling now, he had at the soup kitchen in Albuquerque. Welling up was the feeling he was becoming a bum—a derelict. His status in society was sinking.

He thought of the pictures in magazines of the famous, bearded, author over in Havana, fishing for marlin in the Gulf Stream on his boat, or sometimes hunting lions in Africa.

That was the life Matt thought his life would be like—as a writer—but he felt it all fading now.

He had not sold any stories to a magazine so far, and to keep going, keep writing and sending them, he wondered if he was like the donkey, who keeps moving forward, trying for the carrot being dangled out in front of him.

"You could always take a newspaper job," he said to himself. "Nah," he said, "that would be selling out—admitting defeat. Quitting."

As he walked now, the walls of the Romero house ahead, his hand bumped the bottle of beer in his jacket pocket, and he thought of opening it for a quick drink.

Suddenly, ahead in the middle of the road, a car appeared. It was a convertible, and the top was down, and over the trunk was a camera, the tripod taped to the metal, where a photographer seemed to be filming two men on motorcycles, fancy chrome motorcycles, following behind.

Matt watched them go past, the chrome glinting in the sunshine as they slowly moved by. He could not recognize either of the motorcycle riders.

"Must be part of that movie outfit," Matt said as they went away into the distance toward Taos. "Hopper and Fonda got the money for stuff like that—wish I had the dough to play around like that."

Following the motorcycles was a tan Ford, and bringing up the rear was a pick-up truck at the end of the group. They were all out of sight now.

When they passed, there was no one talking; only the sounds of the motorcycles: that struck Matt as odd.

"Maybe they're stand-ins," Matt said, thinking. "Neither of those guys riding was Hopper—or Fonda. Or maybe, they were testing the camera—or something."

In his apartment, Matt was changing into his painting pants, sipping from the beer bottle, when he decided to open the large manila envelope with his returned story.

Picking up the envelope off the table, he shook his head at the amount of postage in the top corner, wishing he had the money now, and with a screw driver, used to open the paint cans, slit open the taped-down flap.

When he opened the flap, a slim piece of paper fluttered out, falling to the floor.

<u>Sorry</u>, <u>not</u> <u>for</u> <u>us</u>, the editor had written in pencil.

Matt stood staring at the note, remembering what he read in a magazine for writers, about a personal note from editors.

The magazine article explained that editors usually sent a standard printed rejection slip with the returned story. But, if they thought the story worthy, and could be sold elsewhere, they would write a comment, a <u>personal</u> note.

Matt smiled, thinking the editor wrote the note, and was in effect, saying the story was not the kind for his magazine. But, he <u>was</u> saying too, some other magazine might buy it.

Putting the strip of paper back in the envelope, Matt said, shaking his head, "There's that carrot out there on the string, again. The bait for me to keep following—keep writing and sending out stories."

He set the large envelope back on the table, and picked up the bottle of beer.

"Okay—I'll keep on writing," he said and drank down all the beer. "But right now—I got to finish painting walls in apartment number four."

CHAPTER 17

Rain was coming down hard, the next morning, as Matt walked into the bar, after running most of the way, holding a plastic trash bag over his head.

"Did you hear what happened to Marci last night?" Alex asked, watching Matt shake the plastic bag to get the water off.

"No," Matt said, walking around the end of the bar, where he draped the wet bag on the cooler, then went for the empties tub, "I worked late to finish the painting—Romero was griping I was taking too long."

"You didn't hear the ambulance? The Sheriff's sirens?"

"I had the television on," Matt said lifting the tub. "I worked to almost midnight," he added, while walking around the end of the bar with the tub in front of him, "and I think I was getting high on paint fumes."

"Marci got cut on her arm and hand," Alex said quietly.

"Who the hell cut her?" Matt said stopping, holding the tub in front of himself for a moment, then setting it on the floor.

The bar was vacant, as it usually was in the early morning.

"It was Pablo," Alex said quietly, leaning forward, elbows on the bar. "The sheriff's out looking for him now."

Remembering Marci talking to Pablo, through the narrowly open door the other night, Matt reasoned they might have had an argument over drugs. It came to him to be silent, not say anything about what he knew.

Instead, he asked, "How bad off is she?"

"She lost a lot of blood, they say," Alex said straightening up, hands on the bar, and looking at the door. "Her daughter was screaming like crazy—when the ambulance took her mother away—to the hospital."

Alex had been looking at Arnold Hovey, the Frame Shop owner and operator, as he came in the door.

"Marci's home now," Arnold said, shaking the wet off his tan raincoat, picking up on the conversation. "I heard she had eleven stitches," he said sliding off the coat, setting it on the barstool next to him, while sliding on the stool in front of Alex.

"A deputy told me her left wrist, inside, was cut, and the hand on that side, was cut across the palm," Arnold added.

"What the hell set Pablo off?" Matt asked, looking down at the tub at his feet. "What made him do it?"

"She told the Sheriff, I heard," Alex said, pouring vodka into a glass of orange juice for Arnold, his usual bar order, "that he came to the door last night—about ten thirty, and when she opened the door a little, he slashed at her."

Arnold, lifting the glass of vodka, added, "the Sheriff said, he thinks she was reaching out the door—when Pablo cut her."

"What would she be reaching out—for?" Matt asked.

"That's what everybody around town wants to know," Alex said picking up the money Arnold set on the bar.

"Drugs," Arnold said, before he took a long drink of his drink.

"It had to be drugs," Alex said turning to put the money in the cash register.

"Damn," Matt said shaking his head slowly, reaching down to pick up the tub, "that Pablo is a vicious bastard."

Carrying the tub to the door, squinting up at the dark sky and falling rain, he said, "He didn't have to do that to Marci—it seems he was punishing her—for something."

Outside, looking across the plaza to the Sheriff's Office, he saw the deputies talking to a man in a yellow raincoat, standing next to a station wagon with a dog in the back.

"Hope they find him quick," Matt said hurrying down the alleyway next to the bar, back to the trash can, the bottles clinking in the tub, his head turned away from the rain, "and—I hope that dog bites him in the ass—Marci didn't deserve that—marijuana or—no marijuana."

After dumping the bottles in the trashcan, he said to himself, "I got to go over and see how she is—soon as I get done here."

Later, while jogging across the wet highway to the short alleyway to Marci's house, he wished he would have bought a pint of whiskey, something for her.

"Damn it anyhow," he said out loud, "I'm getting tired of being broke all the time—living without money."

Karen opened the front door. She was wearing a tight black jersey, over a pair of fitted black slacks, and Matt stood for a moment, taking in her sleek form.

"Hi," she said smiling, catching his stare, calmly.

"Hi," he said. "How's Marci doing?"

"She's in the studio."

Marci was sitting on the couch, wearing a yellow sweater, her left arm in a sling, her hand at the end, a ball of bandages.

"Hey," Matt said walking over to her, "I just heard at the bar about what happened to you—everybody's worried about you."

"It happened so fast," she said looking up. "I still can't believe it." Then, her head to one side, she said, "This could have been you—with all this—if you'd of been here—answered the door."

Matt stood for a moment, unsure of what to say.

"Have a drink," Karen said as she sat down slowly at the end of the couch. "Join the party—after you take off that wet jacket."

A half bottle of Hennessy cognac sat on the low table in front of the couch; it was plain to Matt they both had been drinking more than they usually do.

"I need a glass," Matt said, backing up to the kitchen, draping his jacket over a wood chair outside the doorway.

In the cabinet above the sink, there was a thick glass with a paper label, ENGLISH CHEDDAR, and he took it.

Out in the studio, he stood pouring cognac in his glass, saying, "You ladies need—a little more cognac?"

"Once a bartender," Marci said, "always a bartender." She held up her glass, "Yes—it's so warm—and soo-thing."

Karen sat up straight, making her breasts and nipples show, the jersey pulling tight, "This is all now, I'm going to run—Kozlo get's testy when I'm away too long."

"He just—doesn't trust you," Marci said, smiling, watching Matt pour cognac in her glass, closely. "Does he?"

"Who could blame him," Matt said, sliding the chair over closer to the couch, his wet jacket on back, dragging on the floor.

"Could be," Karen said, leaning back, holding her drink, "but when he gets done painting for the day—he likes to—have me—nearby. To talk."

"That's a good one," Marci said, shifting her sling to rest on a pillow at her side. "Do you and him—<u>talk</u>—face to face?"

"Uh-huh," Karen said grinning at Marci. "Sometimes."

Matt drank half his glass of cognac, then leaning forward in his chair, asked, "How come Pablo came here last night? Was he high—on something? What—brought him—here?"

Karen sat up quickly, catching Matt looking, "I—think I'll get going—let you two talk."

"Finish your drink, babe," Marci said. "You brought it—it's <u>your</u> cognac."

"I've had enough," Karen said. "You know I don't drink much anyhow."

Matt tired not to let her see him watching, when, after setting her glass of cognac on the low table, she smoothed her tight slacks over her things with her hands.

"Maybe," Matt said to her, "you could call Kozlo—and tell him—because it's raining so hard—you'll be a little late."

He was feeling the warm cognac inside now, and he liked looking at Karen.

"You better let her go, Matt," Marci said, before sipping her cognac.

"I just thought—" he started to explain.

"There's been a lot of—excitement—around here, lately," Marci said. She held up her sling arm. "We don't need more."

Matt shrugged, he was not sure if it was Marci talking, or the cognac.

Karen walked close to his chair when she was moving away, and he felt the warmth of her.

"Call me later," Marci said to Karen when she was over near the front door. "Well—tomorrow for sure."

"Okay," Karen said, putting on her quilted jacket. Then, when she opened the door, she said, "Bye, everybody," and closed the door softly.

"Matt, you better quit bird-dogging Karen," Marci said in an even rolling tone that made her seem more knowledgeable. "You can't even begin—to afford her. Quit looking at her, it's getting obvious—to everyone—what you're after. You better—ease off."

"You're right—in one sense," Matt said, getting up while holding his glass of cognac, then sitting down on the couch, next to Marci, "I can't afford anything right now. But maybe—my book will sell—and I'll make some money." He took a drink of cognac, then added, "All I have to do is finish—writing it."

"Matt, with you it's <u>always</u> maybe," Marci said putting her good hand on his thigh. "Don't you understand you have to live right now too? Do you ever think about that?"

"Yeah, I think about it," he said, leaning his shoulder against hers. "The painting job at Romero's—was just a onetime bonanza. And at the end of the month—I'm right back in the hole again. Broke." He sipped cognac for a moment, then said. "I've got to break out of this circle—just going around and around—somehow."

"You should move in here," she said moving her hand on his leg, "and we'll work something out."

Nodding, as if considering, but knowing he would not, he said, "We'll see."

"You know," Marci said, leaning forward to put her glass of cognac on the low table in front of them, "Pablo wouldn't come around here—like he did the night he came with a knife—if you were here."

Matt almost smiled, listening to Marci's pitch about danger, knowing she would say anything to make him move in.

"You don't think," Matt said, a little dizzy with cognac, "that you bringing the Sheriff's deputy home—the night before—had anything to do with it? You don't think that Pablo jumped you—because he thought you spilled the beans about your deal—to let him hide in the furnace room? You don't think—Pablo figured the deputy was playing you for information?"

Marci sat straight, "That deputy's wife has leukemia," she said. "We started talking at the bar—then came here."

"I talked to the Sheriff at the hospital," Marci said, "when they were bandaging me after the stitches. I told him, Pablo must have thought I had something to do with Hector getting shot on my doorstep—the night of the paint-party."

She waived her good hand.

"Like I turned Hector away—before the deputies shot him. That I wouldn't let him hide here."

"That's crazy-thinking, Marci, and what's worse—you <u>almost</u> believe it. I sure don't—I don't believe any of it."

"I'm not crazy," she said leaning against Matt. "I'm more—vulnerable—than crazy. Don't you think?"

Her face was near Matt's, and he could smell cognac.

"Available—is more like it," he said and kissed her.

She unzipped her slacks.

"Help me, honey," she said, sliding down her slacks. "Pull them off—for me."

She was using her good hand, but could not get them off.

"What—about the kids?" Matt asked her, while helping.

"They're over at Elizabeth's friend's house—her friend's mother has the baby," Marci said holding her sling-arm up, then her rump, helping Matt in removing the slacks. "They'll be back in the morning."

"Careful with that arm," Matt said when he was moving to lay out on the couch. "You might open the wounds."

"I can put it—up—like this," she said, moving the arm next to her head, as she lay back.

"Don't—don't be careful—Matt," she whispered in between taking deep breaths, "Go, boy, go."

* * *

They had made love twice, and Marci slept for twenty minutes after, with Matt watching her breath, smelling the cognac. It had all been good for her, he thought smiling.

When she opened her eyes, she smiled, looking at his face.

"We're good together, Matt," she said in her throaty voice, "and you know we should—be together. Give up your writing—for a while."

"I've got to finish my book," he said to the side of her face. "It's coming along pretty good now."

"But it's wasting your time," she said turning to face him. "We don't have to get married," she said, and in a whisper added, "just be together."

"I've got some time now," he said, "the rent paid for—by the painting job—for this month. I can write steady now for a while—and finish—"

"It's wasting your life, Matt. You're not getting anywhere. You're not making any money."

"Look, I came to Taos," he said, "because it's a place artists live. And I thought, the people here understood a writer needs time—to do his writing."

"But it's not panning out, honey," she said looking up at the skylight for a moment, "and you're just wasting your life."

Matt raised his eyebrows while thinking.

"You're right," he said, "more than you know—my short story just came back from a magazine—rejected."

"See what I mean, Matt?"

"Yeah," he said quietly, "but I'm just—learning the business—I need a little more time."

"Don't you see what it's doing to your life, honey?" Marci moved her sling arm, resting it on her stomach. "You can't go on thinking like that."

"I don't want to give up," he said, rising up to reach over Marci for his cognac glass on the low table. "It's what I want to do—I like doing it."

"What is your short story about?" Marci asked in a skeptical tone, as she watched him sipping the cognac. "Tell me."

"It's not the kind of story you would—be interested in," he said.

"If you sent it out to be published," she said in a deep throaty voice, "you shouldn't be afraid to tell it to me."

"You're right there," he said. "I guess you got me."

"Let me hear the story," she said taking his glass for a sip, and handing it back, "so I can see what's so important to you—that you have to live like a bum."

"Well," Matt began, during World War II a German family moved on our street in Detroit." He lay back, looking up at the rain falling on the skylight, holding the cognac glass on his chest.

"The son, Klaus, was older than most of us kids, he was high school aged. He combed his hair straight back from his forehead. Blond hair. And he was a wizard in the classroom, and said the level of requirements to pass were 'childish,' by German standards. He passed all classes with the highest marks. And the girls were all ga-ga over him."

"I can't imagine why," Marci said. "Go on. Go on."

"Well, maybe this was because his mother taught at a university, somewhere in Germany—and so did his father. We never saw the father, but the mother worked in downtown Detroit, and we saw her walking from the bus stop every day. She walked in an odd way, taking long, gliding strides, like someone on skis.

And like I said, we never saw the father, but I remember someone telling me later, that he 'worked for the government.'"

"When are you going to start the story part, Matt?" Marci asked, before she sat up and took another sip from his cognac glass.

"I'm giving you the background—be patient," he said, taking the glass back.

"Sorry, Matt. I'm listening. Go on, honey," she said and laid back down slow, her sling arm over her chest.

"They had a giant of a dog, a Great Dane, named 'Blanka.' Us kids had never seen a dog as big as Blanka. When it put its paws on the fence gate in the yard, it could look right into a man's face."

"Yikes," Marci said quietly.

"The dog ate a lot, Klaus told us, but I don't remember how much. I do remember, on the hot summer days, Blanka always took a nap in the afternoon on the garage floor, out of the sun. Klaus would have to cover Blanka with gunny sacks to keep the flies off."

"Matt, is all this <u>background</u> necessary, honey?"

"Okay, Marci, here's the story. One day the German family's house was broken into. In broad daylight."

"The dog?" Marci said turning to Matt, "I thought you said the dog was in the yard?"

"The crooks poisoned Blanka—the cops found him back by the alley gate. The crooks must have come in that way to the house."

"Damn," Marci said, taking hold of Matt's arm with her good hand. "Don't stop—tell me the rest."

"The inside of the house," Matt said looking at her, "was all ransacked. The crooks had gone through all the drawers and cabinets, upstairs and downstairs. I heard the father's desk was all pulled apart, and his books on the shelves, all scattered on the floor."

"That sounds like the crooks were looking for something," Marci said, looking at Matt, turning her head on the pillow.

"The FBI came later and looked around the house," Matt said. "You're right, Marci, the crooks <u>were</u> looking for something. Because later, word got around the neighborhood, that German agents—had faked a robbery—to ransack the house."

"Why?" Marci said in a whisper.

"I heard the father, the college professor over there in Germany someplace, was against Hitler's politics and was working with some group—underground—against the Nazis. Somehow, our government brought him here to Detroit."

"What were the German agents looking for?" Marci asked. "That family was really in danger—that's terrible."

"We heard later, around the neighborhood, the Nazi agents were looking for the father's notes, or any papers, about the underground over in Germany."

"What happened after?" Marci asked.

"A few weeks later," Matt said taking a sip of cognac, "over in Germany, they tried to kill Hitler with a bomb planted in his headquarters. But it didn't get him—he lived. And then the German family disappeared, and someone told me the government moved them away," Matt said quietly. "Then, about a year later, a neighbor lady friend of the mother, got a card saying they were living in Arizona, someplace, and that Klaus was in the Air Force."

"Hey, Matt, that's a pretty scary story."

"Yeah, the whole thing scared me, back during the war, because Hitler could reach all the way from Berlin, to a house on our street, five doors down from ours."

"But—the story—Matt, you couldn't sell it?"

"No. It was rejected by the magazine."

Two loud knocks came suddenly at the front door, and Matt and Marci looked at one another.

CHAPTER 18

"Who the hell?" Matt whispered, looking in the direction of the door. "Who could— it be?"

Marci sat up in the bed.

"It's too early for the girls to come home," she whispered, getting dressed with her good hand.

Moving quickly, Matt pulled his t-shirt over his head, then reached for his pants on the floor.

"If it's that damn Pablo again—I'll bust—" he started to say, thrusting his leg into the pants.

"Go see—" Marci interrupted.

Barefoot, he tiptoed across the floor, and looked out the door window, without moving the curtain.

"Elliott," he said in a coarse whisper. Then moving back to the bed, he said, "What's he doing—here?"

Marci, dressed now, pulling on her quilted jacket, said, "Matt, you got to go out the back door—quick."

"It's pouring rain out there," he said sitting down on the bed, then putting on his shoes.

"Matt," Marci said, standing, smoothing her hair back, looked down and, whispering, pleaded, "don't mess up my chance with Elliott. Please—please go out the back—so he doesn't see you."

"Okay, okay," he whispered back.

Picking up his jacket, he was silent, as he walked to the archway that opened into the back of the house.

There were three hard raps on the door.

"Go quick," Marci whispered, walking backward to the door.

Outside, the rain had let up slightly, but the dark clouds still hung overhead menacingly, threatening another downpour.

Matt, by coming out Marci's back door, was on a street a block north of the Taos Plaza. Across the highway was the Taos Hotel.

He hunched in his jacket, crossing the highway, glad it was warmer now, most of the snow gone, except in the mountains.

Once across the highway, he walked on the edge of the roadway, back to the town Plaza.

At the corner, the supermarket was lighted up inside, people going in and out, and as Matt passed, Arnold Hovey came out, carrying two grocery bags.

"Hey, man," Arnold said, "how's Marci doing?"

"She'll be all right," Matt said, while spotting the neck of the quart bottle of Smirnoff vodka in Arnold's grocery bag. "But it's a hell of a place to get cut—on the hand."

"<u>Any</u> knife cut can be hell," Arnold said, quietly. "But I hear, they got that bastard, Pablo—"

"No kidding—when?" Matt said folding his arms.

"The State Police picked him up down in Las Cruses early this morning I heard—at his cousin's place."

"Good news," Matt said, smiling, unfolding his arms. "Marci will be happy to hear that—so will everybody in Taos."

"Yeah, the whole town can breath—easier," Arnold said catching Matt, again, looking at the vodka bottle. "Hey, you going over to tell Marci the news?"

"I can't—Elliott showed up at the door," Matt said, looking out across the plaza. "I had to sneak out the back door," he said smiling, "about twenty minutes ago."

"That Elliott is an idiot," Arnold said while shifting both the shopping bags, "he's got a wife and kids. He's putting his head on the chopping block—with Marci—he's asking for it."

"I know," Matt said, "but Marci got all excited when he knocked at the door, this time, and she thinks—he's going to stay. She even booted me out—the back door."

Arnold grinned, distorting the slack skin of his lower face into a hideous mask. His face matched his wrinkled raincoat, making him look like someone who sleeps in a bus station.

"Ah—h, there's only one Marci," Arnold said. "Hey, come over to the shop—I bought a jug of vodka."

"That's the best offer I got today," Matt said. "What happened—somebody pay up what they owe the shop?"

"Nah, I got an advance from Kozlo—and I been working like a dog. He's having an exhibit—in San Francisco—he brought in eleven paintings he wants framed. I've been working like mad the last two days—and I finished up late last night."

"Didn't the kid help out?" Matt asked.

"Nah, he's got to sleep—be ready for school. Late night stuff is out for him.

I bought him one of those frozen pizzas," Arnold said, looking in the bag opposite the vodka one.

"That will keep him happy while we have the vodka—that and the television."

"I thought you might have spent the day in the bar," Matt said, as they began walking, fishing for a word about Arnold's lady friend.

"Hell no," Arnold said, "I was helping Kozlo pack all those damn paintings in his rented truck—most of the afternoon."

Matt smiled, for thinking Arnold might have been with the lady who owns the stationary story. He spent a lot of time with her; she was plump but had a pleasing, easy manner that made her attractive.

Alex had told Matt at the bar, that rumors in town, were that Arnold was "sweet" on Ilse Petz. She was a widow.

"It's going to be along drive—to 'Frisco,'" Arnold said, "slow—out to California. But, hell, Kozlo don't have much choice—if he wants to get his paintings there—safe and sound."

Matt nodded, remembering once, Arnold told him at the bar, that his wife died of cervical cancer when they lived out in Oakland, California, but after that he never spoke of it again.

Arnold had his teenage son from that marriage, who was retarded.

At the corner, before they walked out of the Taos Plaza, Matt looked across to the Sheriff's Office. Standing in the doorway was that man who looked like Peter Lorre.

"That guy in the raincoat," Matt said to Arnold, "sure spends a lot of time at the Sheriff's."

"I hear he's from the government," Arnold said as they stepped off the curb, leaving the town plaza. "I heard some women at the laundromat talking, that he's doing some sort of survey for the Indian Affairs Department."

"Alex says he was at Acoma last Sunday when we were there," Matt said as they stopped on the street to let a truck pass.

"He must have been surveying the Indians at Acoma," Arnold said, shifting the two grocery bags up higher.

"On a Sunday?"

"Maybe he's a dedicated public servant," Arnold said looking up the street to the houses. "I heard the women in the laundromat say his name—it sounded like Toulouse-Lautrec, but without the Toulouse part, and more the Lautrec."

"I've sene that guy's face," Matt said, squinting, "someplace—but I can't remember—"

"Yeah," Arnold said, quietly, "he does look a little on the shifty side. Kind of—spooky—like Peter Lorre."

They crossed the roadway to a string of houses, behind the Taos Plaza, where Arnold's live-in frame shop was located.

A long sign hanging from the porch ceiling by hooks: TAOS FRAME SHOP distinguished Arnold's house from the others.

"Speaking of movies," Matt said, "how's the movie going with that Hopper guy and his motorcycle?"

"The whole crew packed up and left," Arnold said. "I hear they went to New Orleans. They had a lot of trouble here—waiting for sunny days—to shoot the movie."

Matt nodded.

"Yeah," Arnold said smiling, "they spent most their time up at Arroyo Hondo—filming those hippies up there."

"I never saw that Fonda guy," Matt said following Arnold up the wood steps to the porch of the frame shop, "just Hopper."

"Me neither," Arnold said opening the door. Then he shouted, Norman—I'm home," when inside the house. "Hopper said he liked Taos," Arnold said walking through the shop workroom to the kitchen door.

Matt stood looking at the scattered tools on the workbench; saws, small hammers, and chisels, were next to pieces of frame wood, cut at odd angles, everywhere, even in the sawdust on the floor. And there was an open can of black paint sitting on the corner vice with a thin brush sticking out.

"Hopper said after the movie is done," Arnold said from the kitchen, "he might move here to Taos—from Los Angeles. I heard him say that in the bar to Alex."

Norman came out of the bedroom in a t-shirt and shorts.

"You been sleeping all this time?" Arnold asked him.

"Yeah," the kid said, scratching his stomach. "You and that Polish guy—kept me awake—last night. All that sawing—hammering."

Norman was big-boned like his father; Matt saw the resemblance even in the face, the slack skin at the jaw, the same as his father's.

"I brought you a frozen pizza," Arnold said to the kid from the kitchen doorway, then turned, and Matt could see him take the vodka bottle out of the bag, then a flat box.

"Oh, that's great, dad," the kid said, grinning, when his father held it up.

"This makes up for keeping you awake last night—right?"

"Right," the kid said reaching for the box. "Terrific."

"I don't have orange juice," Arnold said to Matt, "but there's some Squirt—vodka and Squirt sound okay?"

"Sure," Matt said, watching Arnold twisting the cap off the vodka bottle.

Arnold paused a moment, watching the kid slide the pizza into the microwave, then set the timer.

"Go get dressed," Arnold said to him, before taking two large glasses from the cabinet and pouring the vodka.

"Okay," the kid said. "Call me when the timer dings," he added while almost leaping for the bedroom.

"You'll hear it," Arnold said, handing Matt one of the glasses after pouring Squirt. "Sit down at the table," he said to Matt.

Sitting across from Arnold, Matt watched Arnold take a long drink from the glass, and did the same. Matt let Arnold drink first, not wanting to act like a rummy in need of a drink.

"Kozlo's girl, Karen," Matt said, looking at his vodka glass, "was at Marci's this morning. She bought Marci a bottle of cognac—to ease the pain. It was half-gone, but I managed to cage a few drinks of it. It was good stuff."

"That Karen," Arnold said setting his glass on the table, leaning forward, "is 'good stuff' too. She was here last night with me and Kozlo—and man, I couldn't stop looking at her."

"Yeah," Matt said quietly, "she's easy to look at."

"She wasn't wearing a bra," Arnold said. "Hell, she doesn't need one; and Kozlo caught me looking at her—a couple of times."

"Yeah," Matt said, "he watches her like a hawk."

"And I got the feeling," Arnold said, leaning more forward over the table, "she's getting tired of being on a short leash."

Ding: the microwave timer sounded.

The kid came out of the bedroom barefoot, tucking into his Levi's a wrinkled orange t-shirt with the print of the Beatles on the front; he was grinning when he said, "I got the whole thing for myself."

When Matt saw Arnold finish the vodka in his glass, he did the same.

Arnold was watching the kid stack one piece of hot pizza on top of another, then taking a wide bite, as he poured more vodka into his glass.

Matt slid his glass across the table for a refill.

"I wonder," he said, "if Kozlo pays Karen a salary," pausing to watch Arnold pour vodka into his glass, "or—does he just giver her money, when she wants to buy something."

"You've been drinking a lot, today, already, haven't you?" Arnold said, holding up the vodka bottle to see how much remained. "You're half-swacked—you been hitting it hard."

"Yeah," Matt said grinning, "I told you I had cognac over at Marci's."

"Norman," Arnold said quietly to the kid, "go watch some television for a while."

"Okay, dad," the kid said, and after stacking two more pizza slices together, tiptoed quickly to the end of the room, and snapping on television, fell back onto the couch.

"I wish I had money like Kozlo," Matt said reaching for his refilled glass across the table, "I'm tired of being broke."

"Hell, you're lucky," Arnold said quietly, "you—you only got <u>yourself</u>—to worry about."

"Hey," Matt said sitting up straight, "I got an idea—I can sell my typewriter—forty bucks, and it's yours."

"What would I do with a typewriter?"

"The kid," Matt said grinning, "he could type papers—for school—or something."

"Nah, you need—to type your book."

"I <u>need</u> forty bucks more."

"You're just swacked. You can't sell your typewriter."

"It's a Hermes Rocket—and it's not very old. It's worth fifty bucks." Matt took a drink. "Will you buy it?"

"Not for fifty bucks," Arnold said looking across to where the kid sat.

"How much then?"

"Twenty."

Matt, grinning, turned away, and looking across the room, saw Norman watching a children's program on television, sitting on the edge of the couch, forward, eating pizza.

"Okay," Matt said, nodding, "I'll bring it over. Give me the twenty bucks."

"You're sure now—you want to sell it?"

"Yeah," Matt said watching Arnold open his wallet.

"You're just going to drink it up," Arnold said handing Matt the twenty-dollar bill. "Then you'll be right back where you started—looking for money again."

"You're right," Matt said folding the bill, putting it in his shirt picket. "But an idea just came to me how to get some money—and maybe I'll buy the typewriter back."

"Well, I hope you know what you're doing," Arnold said taking a drink from his glass, "that is ain't the booze talking. I ain't sure," he said leaning back in his chair, "who's the bigger idiot—you—or that Elliott chasing Marci."

"Aw-w relax," Matt said, "I just need a few bucks to carry me until I get some money."

"You keep drinking the way you are," Arnold said, "and you're headed for a clinic to dry out. It happened to me—back when I was a musician—after I lost my wife. Believe me, I know."

"Hey," Matt said grinning, "you were a musician?"

"Yeah, in L.A.—I played clarinet in a band."

"How the hell did you wind up in Taos?"

"My wife's brother is an artist—a painter," Arnold said taking a quick sip of vodka, "and he does frame work—for a sideline—to make steady money. I worked for him—off and on—for cash under the table—when he got big jobs.

Then he got wind of this house and shop out here in Taos—it was for sale. He told me with all the painters out here, a frame shop would be a steady business—and I'd have the house to live in."

"So that's when you moved to Taos from Los Angeles?"

"I was living in Oakland when my wife died, and I had the kid to support—and musician jobs were scarce in the San Francisco bay area. I took my wife's insurance money—and moved out here."

Matt, sipping vodka, looked over at the kid.

"Shouldn't he be in school?"

"He was awake most of the night with the noise we made doing Kozlo's frames," Arnold said looking in his vodka glass, "so I let him skip school today."

Matt nodded. "Well, I got to get on my horse," he said standing up. "I got to do some things—so I'm going to go."

"You're half in the bag, Matt."

"Just feeling good."

"Take a slice of pizza—that'll soak up some of the booze in your stomach," Arnold said slow.

Matt took a slice and walked across the room to the front door.

"Thanks for everything, you guys," he said making a salute with the slice of pizza.

"Don't spend the twenty," Arnold shouted back from the kitchen, "all in one place." Then after a pause, he added, "You <u>sure</u> you want to sell—your typewriter?"

Matt nodded, closing the door.

*   *   *

A light rain was falling when Matt stood, breathing heavy from the jog to the apartment, unlocking the door.

In the dark, before putting on the lights, he turned to look back over the wall, to look at the well, only an outline in the lights from the barrio houses.

"Yep," he whispered, "that's the place—for the money. Four rifles—to be exact—worth eight, nine, maybe a thousand bucks. And Pablo won't need them—when he goes to jail."

He closed the door, and snapped on the light.

On the table near the window, he looked for a moment, at the small typewriter. A page lying limp in the roller was part of his book. At the far end of the table, the big manila envelope lay, the top ripped open; that was the rejected story.

"I've come this far," he said slow, "and I'm not going to give up—I couldn't—if I wanted to."

He smiled, looking at the stack of book pages.

"To hell with—selling—the typewriter," he said, and sat down on the bed, then laying back, still wearing his wet jacket, he closed his eyes and fell asleep.

The cognac, vodka, and the twenty dollars, had given him relief from confronting his money problem for the day.

CHAPTER 19

A wind had come up, and the hissing sound it made blowing the rain, woke Matt up. Turning on the light, he looked at the small alarm clock on the bed table; one twenty-one AM.

"Time to go to work," he said to himself.

Slipping off his damp jacket, he dug out his dark blue sweatshirt from the pile of clothes on top the dresser, and while pulling it over his head, grinned, when he saw the yellow word MICHIGAN across the chest.

After turning off all the lights, he went to the small window over the sink. Outside, he could see the warm rain was raising a mist from the cold ground.

"Perfect," he whispered, walking to the front door. "You couldn't ask for better cover for what I got to do."

Moving quickly across the back yard, running hunched and low, he reached the back wall dark spot. He had found this dark place on the wall, after first looking at the angle of light coming from the Romero house back door floodlight. On the barrio side of the wall, this corner was in the dark angle also. It was perfect cover.

Quickly climbing over the wall, he stayed in the shadow all the way over to the well.

Bending to reach over the edge of the well wall, the stone pressing against his stomach, he searched with his hands for an opening.

It was not until he reached so far down, that he nearly fell over the edge, he found the jagged opening of a crevice, then the corner of a plastic bag.

Grinning with satisfaction, he brought up the first bundle, and could feel they were plain rifles. The second package held the rifles with telescopic sights, he could feel them through the plastic wrapper, and he grinned widely.

Keeping in the shadow, he climbed slowly over the wall, after setting both bundles on top, next to where he slid over the top.

He was surprised no neighborhood dogs had started barking, and grinned while taking the two bundles off the wall.

"Bingo," he said to himself, waking in the dark to his apartment door, "this is a thousand dollar night."

By daybreak the next morning, the rain had stopped, but the wind grew gusty, making the sky a jumble of white and gray moving clouds.

Matt woke up feeling good about the prospect of the day, despite the dry mouth and the burn in his hangover stomach. He looked at the wet sweatshirt he draped over the back of a chair last night, and smiled. It was his lucky sweatshirt; it served him at the well when he found the hidden rifles.

After setting a pan of water on the stove to heat, he sat down at the table. Picking up a spoon, he ladled out a heaping spoon of coffee from the near-empty Maxwell House instant coffee jar into one of the cheap mugs that came with the apartment's furnishings for the kitchen.

For a moment, he looked at the sweatshirt again, remembering wearing it on his trip to Spain.

He was trying to write in Spain last spring. He wore the sweatshirt in the morning, when he left the Pension Fe on Claudio Cuello Avenue in Madrid, and walked to the park—The Retireo—and sat on a bench near the lake. He spent most of the day on the bench scribbling his stories in a notebook. The warm sun made it easy to sit there.

One day, a movie company began filming across the lake, in front of the marble buildings, over there in the background. The actors were all dressed like Mandarin Chinese, but he never found out what the movie was about—the story.

Smiling, he remembered he wore the sweatshirt in the bar on the Spanish island, Ibiza. He met two wealthy American girls at the bar, that were students in a ritzy school in Switzerland, and they drank so much, they all ended up in the bed at their apartment—laughing and wriggling—until the clothes came off.

He wore the sweatshirt when he moved from Ibiza to the smaller island, Formentera, where rent for a farmhouse was thirty dollars a month. These were the Balearic Islands of Spain.

His writing all day impressed the peasant family, who owned the house on Formentera, and they let him join them for supper at their house. After a while, Matt remembered giving them fifty cents each time he ate there. He had learned to eat pigeon, rabbit, and a fish called "calamari."

In the evening on the island, Matt remembered wearing the sweatshirt to town. The small, dusty town, San Francisco de Xavier, where the only bar was the Fonda Pepe.

When the water in the pan began boiling, Matt went to the stove across the cold floor of the apartment, and came back to fill the coffee cup—almost in a trance from thinking about Spain.

It was in Spain, he remembered, that he first felt he was being watched.

He sat thinking at the table, stirring the instant coffee, about who it could be watching—and why.

"The only answer," he said out loud, "it's the army. It <u>has</u> to be the army—they're the ones watching me."

His reasoning was backed up, now, buy an incident that happened at the bar—the Fonda Pepe—there on Formentera.

He sat, sipping the scalding coffee, thinking back, recalling the day he sat at the bar, and a load of tourists climbed off the island bus outside the Fonda door. The tourists were mixed with the village locals, returning home from the big island, Ibiza.

All the tourists, it later came out, were army personnel, on leave. They said they were stationed in Stuttgart, all five of them.

Matt remembered when he joined them at a table in the Fonda, telling he had served in Wurzburg, and talking about life in the army, one of the group, a negro girl, stout, wearing a sweatshirt with the logo, MARYLAND, continually watched him.

He looked away several times, he remembered, and every time he looked at her, he saw her eyes studying him. It made him uneasy—it were as if she was telling him something—and it was not good.

It lead him to ask the question, why would five army personnel show up in a bleak village on a small island off Spain.

His only answer, he could tell himself, was that it had something to do with his contracting Tuberculosis while stationed in Germany.

Matt had caught the disease while serving during his year and a half in Germany. At the camp dispensary, the German doctor kept stalling him, even threatening him with reporting him for malingering, for his persistence about feeling sick.

Later, while on leave, Matt went to the large army hospital in Frankfort, and requested an x-ray, he remembered, and they found that he had the disease. He was flown home, discharged from the army, and was treated at the Veterans hospital in Detroit. A year later, he enrolled at college.

Several times, while attending classes at the university in Detroit, he had the feeling he was being observed—but he shrugged the thought away, enjoying the heavy beer drinking sessions in campus bars with fellow students.

He nodded, thinking about another suspicious incident, here in Taos, just a few days after he arrived.

A girl appeared at the bar, saying she was a tourist and when Alex asked her what kind of work she did, she said she was a first reader for a major publishing company. She read books submitted by writers, and if they were worth consideration for being published, she would forward the books to senior editors for a decision to print it or not.

Matt remembered telling the girl, Doris, between drinks, that he had submitted his first book to Harper Publishing Company. This was before he worked for Alex, and was a customer.

When she said she recalled reading it, he knew she was lying. He had the feeling she was following him—all this talk about publishing was <u>too</u> coincidental—most, her being in Taos.

Sitting at the table, sipping coffee, he saw a pattern of being followed—if you knew how to look—and he nodded, thinking. That was not all, people were suspicious of writers.

Trying to break into publishing—made crooks out of some writers. The rest—who tried, honestly, to break into the business—were regarded as troublemakers, and at best, oddballs, and outcasts.

Matt could sympathize with Irving, who wanted a big book sale, who wanted to make his name famous, and make himself financially secure—and what was pushing him to write a phony biography of Howard Hughes.

Shaking his head, Matt could not excuse Irving from involving Ellspeth into his failed scheme. She was the woman Matt had seen Irving with on Ibiza, who Matt knew from the King George, an English bar on Ibiza, and where he had a fit of sneezing, while sitting next to her at the bar, where she told him she was Swiss, married to a toy manufacturer and had a daughter, and handed him a lace handkerchief to wipe his nose.

Irving duped Ellspeth into posing as Helga Hughes, who, wearing a black wig, tried cashing the giant check from the publishing company, hoodwinked into believing Irving had given them the definitive biography of Howard Hughes.

But the scheme backfired, and when Ellspeth was arrested, she spoiled the whole scheme Irving concocted to police. There were photos in LIFE magazine; Irving was tried, and sent to Federal prison.

Sitting at the table in his damp apartment, Matt stretched, thinking of the longing for success everybody has, what lead Irving to do what he did. How could he blame Irving; everybody wants recognition for the work they do.

Grinning, Matt stood up, dropping the spoon into the coffee cup, the <u>plinking</u> sound filling the room.

"Time to go to work," he said to himself. Then, looking around the room, added, "Got to find a box—or carton—for the rifles—to carry them in."

When there was nothing available in the apartment, he went to the front door and looked out. At the end of the building, under the portico roof, was the trash pile outside apartment four, now being refurbished by Romero.

On top of a box marked AIR CONDITIONER, set another empty box marked DRAPERY RODS, that was flat, and about four feet long.

"Hey," he said picking up the flat box, shaking the wrapping paper out, "this will work fine."

Back in the apartment, he slid the rifles out from under the bed. They were still wrapped in black plastic bags. He liked the <u>feel</u> of the telescopic sights while he was laying the bags in the long box; they felt expensive—worth a lot of money.

Instead of the direct way to the Taos Plaza, he took the side road route, walking the streets lined with houses. Passing the Frame Shop, he grinned, thinking of the vodka drinking session, and the selling of the typewriter. The flat box of rifles he carried on his right shoulder would change everything.

Coming up to the parking lot behind the bar, he saw Alex's Thunderbird. Looking around to see if anyone was near, he stepped up to the car, opening the door, he reached inside to pull the trunk lever and heard it pop open. He set the flat box next to the spare tire in the trunk.

"I'll bring you inside later," he said to the rifles before slamming the trunk lid.

Even before Matt closed the bar front door, Alex said from behind that bar, "Things are quiet now—I'm going to run to the bank."

"Right," Matt said, unzipping his jacket, passing Alex coming around the end of the bar, carrying the cash bag.

"The Budweiser truck comes today," Alex said pulling open the front door. "About noon."

"All right," Matt said walking up behind the bar, "I'll clear the hallway to the storeroom."

Matt shrugged, because there was no back door to the bar, all the beer deliveries had to be carried through the front door.

Alex stopped, holding the door open, "Ah-h, I got some—important news," he said looking over his eyeglasses. "I'll fill you in—when I come back," he added, as if, on second thought, he did not want to say what it was.

Waiting a minute after Alex was out the door, Matt picked up the tub of empty bottles under the bar, and dashed out.

After dumping the bottles into the trash can in one swift move, Matt opened the trunk of Alex's car, and carrying the flat box on top of the tub, hurried back into the bar.

In the narrow closet, he slid the flat box down on the bench, next to the vacuum cleaner, away from the mops in the corner, and the bottles of soap, disinfectant, and window cleaner on the floor.

Out in the bar again, Matt was stacking beer bottles in the cooler, when Kozlo came in the door.

"Has Karen been in here?" he asked, pronouncing the first part of her name like the word "car."

"No. I haven't seen her today," Matt said, continuing stacking beer bottles, but watching Kozlo, as he slowly sat down on a barstool.

Up close, Matt saw that his bulbous nose was even more prominent, like a peasant's, along with his thick hands on the bar.

With his barrel chest, and short legs, he gave a sturdy appearance, like someone who could work on a farm all day. He did not look like an artist—a painter, who created pictures with graceful angels floating in the sky above Slavic villages, Matt thought to himself.

"Give me a vodka—with orange juice," he said politely.

"Sure," Matt said, and after drying his hands on a bar towel, picked up the Smirnoff bottle from the back bar. "This is the good stuff," he said smiling.

"The best vodka—is made from potatoes," Kozlo said, as if remembering from long ago. "This is grain alcohol."

Pouring the vodka into a glass, half-filled with orange juice, Matt said, "I hear you're heading to California."

"That's right," Kozlo said, and after taking a drink from the glass, leaned back to look out the window at his rented truck parked across the plaza. "Karen is saying goodbye to Marci—and I am waiting. When she comes—we go."

Nodding, Matt, to keep from smiling at Kozlo's words, went back to stacking bottles in the cooler, and then, suddenly he saw the Budweiser delivery truck roll up at the curb outside the window.

Matt hurried around the end of the bar to the front door, and as he was putting the stopper to hold it open, the driver came up holding an order bill, "You ordered thirty cases, right?"

"The boss will be here in a minute," Matt said, "he'll okay it. But I counted twenty-nine empty cases in the store room."

"I'll load them first," the driver said. "I'll get the hand cart."

Matt, walking back to turn on the lights in the pool room, that served as a storeroom too, heard a woman say, "Gregory—a policeman is writing a parking ticket on your truck," from the open door.

Matt saw Karen in the back bar mirror and turned. "Ah-h," he said, grinning. "California or bust, hey?"

"Elliott is back at Marci's," she said, but Kozlo, quick off the stool blocked her from saying more, by taking her arm muscle with his hand, turning her as he walked out the doorway.

"Have a nice trip," he shouted, grinning, while reaching to turn on the light in the poolroom. Then quipped to himself, "Must be in a hurry."

Matt stood counting the empty cases the driver took, then with the last load, followed the driver out into the bar.

He picked up Kozlo's half-full vodka glass, and drank it down, then set the glass in the sink under the bar.

Alex came in following the driver, wheeling the first load of cases with full bottles.

"I only need twenty cases," Alex said to the driver. "Only leave twenty, today."

"How come?" the driver said, stopping. "The order says thirty—did the office get it wrong?"

"I may not be open," Alex said looking over the bar at Matt.

"Are you serious?" Matt asked.

Leaning on the edge of a barstool, Alex said, "That's what I meant, when I said I had something important to tell you today—I've decided to put the bar up for sale."

CHAPTER 20

"How come all of a sudden you want to sell the bar?" Matt asked, fighting back disbelief. "I mean—why?"

"The damn landlord," Alex said, pushing his eyeglasses up higher on his nose, "hiked the rent up—a quarter more than what I'm paying now. He says because of the pool room—that I'm using more room in the building."

"That bastard," Matt said, looking at the Budweiser delivery man, who was listening.

"The rent would be higher," Alex said, "than what I take in—including the pool room. I'd be loosing money every month."

"Damn," Matt said, shaking his head. "Did you tell him that? Explain that to him?"

"Yeah, and he says the extra room I'm using has to be paid for," Alex said, shrugging. "So there it is in a nutshell."

Matt sensed Alex was not too upset about selling the bar, and watching him, he read quite the opposite; Alex seemed relieved in some way.

Matt was thinking of making a remark about losing his job at the bar, but instead, reached down into the cooler for his one free beer for the day.

Opening the beer, he said, "I got a bit of news too—"

But Alex and the Budweiser driver had moved to the end of the bar, so Matt stopped talking.

Alex took a tablet sized checkbook folder from under the bar, then wrote a check, while sitting on the end stool.

Handing the check to the driver, he said, "If things change, I'll call your office."

"Right," the driver said, and went out the door.

After taking a drink from the beer bottle, Matt said, "Elliott showed up at Marci's this morning. Or should I say, the idiot showed up at Marci's. I don't know if that's news or not."

"Some guys never learn" Alex said while putting the check folder back under the bar. He was grinning. "He's really asking for trouble this time. With four kids, yet. His wife will wipe him out—leave him penniless."

Matt was taking a long drink of beer, and near choked, seeing Elliott walking past the front window, then coming in the open door.

"Speak of the devil," Matt said watching Elliott.

Elliott came in and quickly sat down on a stool near the window.

"How's Marci doing?" Matt asked, wiping the surface of the bar with a towel, trying to sound as if he has not seen her. "She healing all right? No infection—anything like that?"

"The wounds won't infect," Elliott said knowingly. "The doctor gave her shots for that," he said and finished the cognac in his glass, then slid his glass toward Matt for a refill.

"Damn that Pablo," Elliott said watching Matt pour cognac into the glass. "If I had my hunting rifle here—he'd never do anything like that again."

Two elderly women, who always seemed to be together, came in the front door and sat down at a table near the end of the bar. They were regular customers.

"Two grasshoppers please," one said as she opened her coat with a fur collar. "We're going to Las Vegas on the bus," she said to Alex, who was already pouring Crème de Menth into the mixture, two tulip shaped glasses on the bar in front of him.

"Ah-h," Alex said smiling, "Lost Wages—Nevada."

"Let's hope not," the second woman, in a black and tan checker coat said, adjusting her pill box hat with her gloved hands.

Both of them sat up erect, knees together.

"I'll serve them," Matt said, silently putting his empty daily beer bottle in the tub, while walking down the bar. Taking two napkins and the tulip glasses, he stepped around the end of the bar.

"Give me a cognac, Matt" Elliott said opening his light tan raincoat. "And don't make any wisecracks—I don't need them—about me and Marci."

Smiling, Matt looked at the expensive tweed sports jacket Elliott wore under the raincoat, and the tattersall shirt, and thought, from now on, with Marci, he would be lucky if he could afford Levis.

"You want a snifter?" Matt asked with a broad grin, while reaching for the cognac bottle on the back bar display.

Alex had drifted down the bar, and was washing glasses in the sink, his head down, and at the 'snifter' remark, made a noise that was half-cough and half-laugh.

"No, no snifter," Elliott said oblivious to the remark. He lifted his left elbow, setting it on the bar, holding the side of his head with his hand. It was obvious to Matt he had been drinking.

Then Elliott said slowly, "What a mess I walked into—over at Marci's house."

Matt nodded, pouring cognac into a glass on the bar, thinking how earlier he had been drinking Marci's cognac, and had gone through the same dilemma with her.

After swallowing half the drink, Elliott said, "Damn, they're all crying over there—at the Ufer House. Elizabeth keeps blubbering about her mother's arm being cut—she's damn near hysterical. Marci's crying because her daughter's so distressed. Hell, even the baby's crying."

Alex smiled; he knew the women always set a dollar on the table when they left, and Matt wanted it.

After setting napkins on the table, then placing the glasses on them, Matt said to the women, "Good luck at the roulette tables in Vegas."

"Oh, we like the blackjack tables," the lady with the fur collar said.

"We count the cards," the checker coat lady said in a soft voice. "And they're on the watch for that—we have to be careful."

"Well," Matt said, "good luck with that too," smiling, watching them lift their drinks, before stepping away.

At the bar, Alex had moved up in front of Elliott, and was drying bar glasses with a towel, when Matt walked up, next to Elliott and said, "I think I'm going to head for home—I got stuff I have to do." Then he whispered, "Keep the grasshopper dollar for me Alex."

"Have a cognac with me," Elliott said turning to Matt. "You're off duty—you're a customer again."

"I don't—" Matt started to say, but Alex, grinning set a glass in front of him on the bar. "Well, okay," he said and climbed on the stool next to Elliott.

"Don't miss the opportunity," Alex said pouring cognac "things change rapidly, you know."

Matt nodded, with Alex saying in a guarded way the bar might be sold soon; he would have to buy his own drinks.

Day customers began filling up the bar.

The tow-truck driver from the gas station, over on the highway, came in and took the seat where the bar curved and ended at the wall. He ordered a shot of tequila and a draft beer.

Three young women, looking like schoolteachers, came in, Matt watching them in the mirror, as they sat down at a table. One carried a large bag with the logo: TAOS ART SUPPLY.

One of the women put money in the jukebox. She played Mexican music with blaring trumpets.

Elliott had two refills of cognac for him and Matt, and when he ordered again, Matt said, "I got to switch to beer—my stomach is burning."

Elliott had been talking in muted tones, telling Matt about his problems with his divorce. Matt nodding, acting interested.

Elliott's wife had hired some expensive lawyer, who had cut him off at the bank and credit cards. He only had the credit card for deposits from his architectural office account now.

That will give Marci a fit, Matt thought, because she thought Elliott would bring his wealth with him.

"What about the house?" Matt said.

"My former wife's working on that," Elliott said, showing the effect of the cognac, leaning his head on his fist, elbow on the bar. "I got the Jeep—but she's got the Buick and the station wagon."

Four young men came in the bar, all wearing athletic jackets. They went back into the poolroom, and there was laughter and wisecracks.

One of the men came out and ordered four beers, standing next to Matt to get the order over the bar from Alex.

Matt held off his next question to Elliott; recalling the photo in Marci's kitchen of Elliott, holding a hunting rifle, running through his mind. He did not want to speak, the young man might hear. Elliott might be interested in buying a rifle; Matt was hoping.

When the young man stepped away with his beer order, Matt asked Elliott, "Your wife get your—hunting stuff?"

"She's got my whole damn gun closet."

Matt took a sip of beer, thinking of his previous deal with Elliott, the six-pack and shot of Jim Beam, and how the agreement was kept from Marci hearing about it.

"Well," Matt said, feeling more confident because Elliott never mentioned the deal, keeping him away from Marci, so he blurted, "if you were serious—when you said—you'd pop Pablo—if you had the chance—"

"Damn right," Elliott said, his words slightly slurred, "he's got it coming—after—what he did to Marci, the bastard."

"Who could blame you," Matt said, feeling more confident now, that he was on the right track.

"I'd put a hole in him—all right," Elliott said, and he sipped a bit more cognac.

"I know a guy," Matt said quietly, leaning toward Elliott slightly, "who's got a rifle for sale. It's brand new—never been fired."

"It's not stolen?" Elliott asked putting his glass down on the bar.

"No—nothing like that."

"What's—what's he asking for it?"

"A hundred seventy-five," Matt said cautiously. "It's just a plain rifle—no telescopic stuff."

"He—wants—cash, right?"

"Yeah, it's that kind of a deal. He needs money—that's why he's selling it."

"I'd feel—a lot better—with a rifle around," Elliott said leaning toward Matt, "over at Marci's studio. Protection—if that Pablo comes around again."

"Okay," Matt said, taking a sip of beer to not appear over anxious, "I'll try to run him down—tonight, maybe, and see if he still has it. I'll tell him you are interested.

"Bring the rifle," Elliot said. "You bring the rifle, Matt, and I'll get the cash from the bank—tomorrow morning—from my office account. Tell him—the sooner the better okay."

"If he still has it," Matt said, to carry on the charade, "I'll bring it here—to the bar in the morning. You can take it home—wrapped in your raincoat."

"What about people," Elliott said attempting to act coherent, "customers in the bar?"

"Nah," Matt said, looking forward at himself in the bar mirror, "the mornings are always slow—besides, they wouldn't know what we're doing."

"I guess you're right," Elliot said, thoughtfully, before taking another sip of cognac. "What caliber is it?"

"Thirty-ought-six, probably," Matt said watching himself drinking beer in the back bar mirror. "I'll check, first thing."

"I don't want a—odd ball caliber."

"I'll check. If it's odd, I won't bring it."

Elliott nodded.

"It'll be nice to have a new gun," he said, titling his head to one side. "Like I'm starting over—with new things."

Matt suddenly realized he was creating fiction with the story he was telling Elliott—for money. The difference here, was he was not writing it down, he told himself, looking in the mirror. He smiled.

In the bar mirror, he saw the Peter Lorre look-alike coming in the door with the woman who owned the antique and art gallery in the hotel lobby.

Matt watched as they sat down at a table near the door, and the woman held up two fingers to Alex behind the bar. In a few moments, he saw Alex take two glasses of white wine to the table, her usual order. She was a regular at the bar.

Sipping his beer, Alex tried remembering where he had seen the Peter Lorre face before. All he could recall, was that is had been recently, he had seen it, someplace.

"You sure," Elliott said, "that this guy selling the rifle—isn't a crook—selling a stolen gun?"

Matt realized the question was telling him Elliott had not heard about the theft of the rifles from the hardware store.

"Oh no," he said to Elliott, and suddenly the drug deal he saw Pablo make at the well, came to mind, so he blurted, "he's a rancher."

"A cattle rancher?"

"No, horses," Matt said, hoping Elliott would believe the story. "He raises and sells horses."

"Doesn't he need a rifle?" Elliott asked. "Doesn't he need—protection around the ranch? Why is he selling—?"

Matt smiled at Elliott's slurred speech.

"He doesn't—have time for hunting these days," Matt said. "He likes deer hunting." Matt was enjoying making up a story again.

"He's a friend of my landlord—at my apartment. They were talking, one day, when I was painting—and he came in with the owner to check on how I was doing. I heard them talk."

The last flurry of fiction seemed to satisfy Elliott, who said, "Okay, I'll come by in the morning—with the money."

"I'll be here," Matt said, sneaking a quick look at the Peter Lorre man, who was beginning to look like a snoop.

Then again, Matt had the sensation, he was being watched.

CHAPTER 21

The next morning, when Elliott saw Alex leave the bar for the bank, he walked across Taos Plaza from his Jeep where he had been watching. Everything was working the way Matt had told him.

"You got the one seventy-five?" Matt asked form behind the bar as Elliott came in.

"Yes," he said shifting his raincoat from one arm to the other, to dig the cash out of his pants pocket. "I was the first customer at the bank this morning."

"Come back to the hallway," Matt said moving quick down to the end of the bar.

Following, Elliott said, "I'm still trying to find out why Pablo cut Marci—it was such a— vicious attack. She just keeps telling me, that she doesn't know."

"Maybe," Matt said, "somebody will get the answer from Pablo—someday."

Matt held back from explaining to Elliott about how Marci let Pablo hide in the furnace room, where the kerosene smell from the storage tank would throw off search dogs. In exchange, Marci got two marijuana joints each week.

Then there was the incident with the Sheriff's deputy, Matt did not want to tell Elliott about either. How Marci met the deputy at the bar, and went home to her place that same night, that after the deputy left, Marci was cut.

Pablo might have thought Marci was informing on him to the deputy.

Matt figured it was best to keep quiet. Let the story leak out, as it was bound to do.

At the closet, Matt pulled the rifle out of the black plastic bag, then handed it to Elliott.

"Ah," Elliot said, "a Remington," as he pulled open the bolt. And reading the inscription on the receiver, said smiling, "It's a thirty odd-six—perfect."

"Keep it down," Matt said. "Don't show it—so somebody can see it." Then, holding out his hand, added, "Give me the money."

"Right here," Elliott said taking the wad of bills out of his pocket again, handing it to Matt. In the excitement of seeing the rifle, he had jammed the money back in his pants pocket.

Matt did not count the money, before sliding it into his pants pocket, while looking out to the bar for Alex, or a customer.

Opening his baggy sports jacket, Elliott raised the rifle by the butt, and slid it down his left pant leg, twisting the butt so it caught on his belt, which would keep it from dropping or sliding out.

"I thought this up last night," he said to Matt, who stood nodding.

When he closed his sports jacket, Elliott held the raincoat on his arm forward, covering his legs from the front; the gun would not be noticed.

Elliott walked with a slight limp, Matt noticed when he followed him out into the bar, but kept silent.

As Matt was pouring cognac for Elliott, Alex came back from the bank.

"Having a cognac breakfast?" Alex said while walking around the end of the bar, then dropping the canvas bag next to the cash register.

"I'm driving Marci to the hospital this morning," Elliott said to Alex, watching Matt slide the cognac glass in front of him. "They want to check her out—and change the bandages."

Putting the cognac bottle on the back bar, Matt had the sudden insight that Marci could tell Elliott about the rifles being stolen from the hardware store. That would create a giant problem; Matt realized he would have to concoct some kind of story, if that happened.

"Marci will be all right—back to her old self—in no time," Alex said, grinning at Elliott. "She's a live wire."

"Hope you're right," Elliott said, and drank the cognac, standing, and put two dollars on the bar, then slowly walked out.

Matt walked down the bar saying, "I'm going to sweep the poolroom—it smells—foul—back there."

"It should be mopped too," Alex said to Matt's back. Then lifting the hard-boiled egg basket on the back bar, added, "All the eggs are sold, and there's a dollar and a quarter under here."

"Right," Matt said turning into the hall, "I'll boil some tonight."

After Matt filled the mop bucket, and was stepping across the hall to the poolroom, he saw a man in a tan ski jacket and tailored gabardine slacks walk in the bar front door. He was carrying a gallon can of paint.

His haircut was tailored too, with just the right amount of gray showing at the temples.

"I'm Colin Bannister," he said to Alex behind the bar, setting the gallon of paint on the bar stool in front of him. "I'm one of the owners of the ski lodge up at Eagle's Nest."

"Good to meet you," Alex said. He had been wiping off the dust on the back bar, moving the bottles, and he stopped, holding the towel in his hands.

"My business partner mentioned you were considering selling the—cantina," Bannister said quietly, glancing out the front window at the plaza.

"Word travels fast," Alex said, lifting his eyeglasses up higher on his nose.

"Taos is a small town," Bannister said, "and the business community—is even smaller. That is to say, my partner informed me that this bar would fit into our plans for a commercial enterprise that is open all-year around. Not just seasonal—like the ski lodge."

"Oh, I see," Alex said, putting down the towel on the bar. "Step to the end of the bar— we can talk—in case a customer comes in. And bring your can of paint."

"It's varnish, actually," Bannister said, lifting the can by the wire handle. "We have a knotty-pine paneled lobby at the lodge, and we're going to brighten it up," he said walking down the bar to the end.

Matt, who had heard the whole conversation, ducked into the poolroom, pushing the mop pail with his foot, as they came to the end of the bar, just opposite the doorway.

The first thing that came to Matt's mind, was, that he better get the rest of the rifles out of the bar. Things at the bar were changing fast, that was for sure.

As he was mopping the floor, he realized that Alex had made the decision to sell, quickly, after the funeral trip up to Michigan; he had the feeling there was more to it than the landlord raising the rent—and maybe Alex's wife had influenced the decision.

"Hey Matt," Alex shouted from out in the bar. Leaning on the mop, Matt looked out the doorway, "We're going to talk to a lawyer across the plaza—you run the bar for a while."

"Okay, I'll hold the fort," Matt shouted back, and when he finished mopping he pushed the bucket into the doorway, and leaned the handle of the mop, so they would block the door until the floor dried.

When he heard the front door open, he walked back behind the bar.

A man and two women, young, college age, came into the bar, looking around at the Mexican decorations on the walls.

The man wore a black hat with a wide brim, and flat top, looking like a Spanish aristocrat.

"We've been on a trip to Mexico," one of the girls said, as Matt was setting their order of marguerites on the table.

Matt smiled and nodded.

"Taos is the town D.H. Lawrence lived in—before he went down to Mexico," the other girl said.

"We're literature students at Kansas University," the man said. "We thought we should stop here—study the atmosphere."

"Yes," Matt said, "a lot of people come here for that same reason."

When the students left, Matt took the loading dolly used for hauling stacked beer cases, set the mop bucket on the bottom platform, the box of rifles on top, upright, then put three pieces of scrap panel wood, cut at odd angles, covering the box.

Out in the back of the bar, he looked for a place to hide the rifles. At the end of the parking lot, he saw the low stack of used telephone poles, that sometimes the Pueblo Indians sat on, drinking whiskey they bought at the supermarket. There were dark spaces between the poles, stacked in the form of a small pyramid, where they lay on top of one another.

Matt slid the flat box of rifles into one of the spaces.

Going quickly over to the trashcan, he set the scrap wood paneling next to the can, then dumped the mop water from the pail.

"That takes care of that—for a while," he said, taking quick steps, pushing the dolly in front of himself. "I've got to come up with someplace I can hide those rifles—permanently," he said, turning out of the alleyway, stepping into the bar door.

Matt began dusting the back bar, moving the bottles, like Alex had been doing, when now, Alex and the ski-lodge owner came in the door.

They were talking in low tones, so Matt did not say anything; he watched as they continued talking, sitting down again on stools at the end of the bar.

Moving the cognac bottle to dust behind it, Matt had the sudden idea to hide the rifles at Marci's, the cognac triggering the thought.

He could hide the rifles in the furnace room, when he got off work. Marci, Elliott, and even Elizabeth and the baby, would all be at the hospital.

Grinning, thinking it would be a dirty trick hiding the guns at her house. It might get her in a lot of trouble if the Sheriff found out, but he had to take the chance. He felt pressed. He had to hide the rifles <u>somewhere</u>.

At least, until he found a better place.

The bar door opened and Monk came in, and behind him, a guy wearing an army fatigue jacket and hat.

The fatigue hat made Matt smile; he had worn one like it back, when he was in the army. It was the same style Castro wears in his photos, at the time he took over Cuba, when he wore a beard and the fatigue hat with the flat side.

"We want to shoot some pool," Monk said, moving to the back of the bar room.

Alex turned away from the ski resort owner, and said over his shoulder, "Matt just mopped back there. It's wet."

"It'll just be a little damp by now," Matt said moving quickly down the bar to the back room.

He removed the mop and bucket left in the doorway of the poolroom, when he had come back from dumping the pail. He put them in the maintenance closet now.

"We won't complain about a littler water," the guy in the Castro hat said.

Matt flinched looking at the guy in the Castro hat; he was the cowboy who had the horse trailer, the one who swapped drugs with Pablo for one of the rifles.

"Matt," Monk said turning on the lights over the pool table, "bring us two beers—and one for yourself."

"I was just about to go," Matt said, trying to think of a reason to leave, "and do my— laundry. I've been putting it off—for two weeks. Thanks—I'll bring your two beers though."

The Castro hat guy was racking the pool balls on the table, and said without looking up, "Come back when you're done. We'll probably still be here."

"It's starting to drizzle outside," Monk said, looking at the rack of pool cues for the one he wanted.

"Maybe—I'll stop by," Matt said, while looking closely at Monk, "when I get done with the laundry. I'll get your beers."

Matt thought, as he walked out to the bar, Monk was too aggressive, not his easy-going self. He must be on something: some drug.

When he brought the two beers, he thought of asking Monk how he knew the Castro guy, but did not get the chance. The Castro hat seemed, always, too near, so he said, "See you, I'm taking off."

Outside, a soft rain was falling and no people were out walking the plaza, and Matt hurried back to the pile of telephone poles. Passing the scrap wood paneling next to the trashcan, he picked up a long piece, and when he slipped the box out of its hiding place, covered the rifle box with the scrap.

"Damn," Matt said walking quickly up the alley to Marci's house, "it looks like that Castro guy <u>knows</u> the rifles are gone from the well—and he's—out hunting around town—looking for them."

"I got to be careful—or I'm going to end up—laying dead—out in some dried up creek bed in the desert."

Inside the furnace room at Marci's, Matt pushed the flat box in the space behind the kerosene tank, where the tank end was close to the wall, the box upright.

Closing the door quickly, he walked back up the alley, looking in all directions, feeling the fear of winding up dead.

The fear started with a tight chest, then went to his stomach, and stayed there.

What made it worse, was not knowing what to do next.

"I'll get a bottle," he said to himself. "Vodka will ease the stomach. I'll go back to my apartment—and think up a plan."

He had no money worries now, he had the hundred and seventy-five from Elliott. He liked the feeling of having money.

Walking toward the Safeway supermarket to get the vodka, Matt suddenly had a vision. He saw the Castro guy, standing at the well, looking at the surrounding buildings, studying them, slowly. When the Castro guy looks over the wall, he gets a good view of the Romero house apartments.

"If he finds out I live in one of those apartments," Matt said as he walked, now, under the portico of the Taos Plaza, his hands in his pockets, thinking, "he's going to come after me. I'm—the logical one—who would have seen the rifles Pablo put in the well crevice—from my apartment."

A deep sense of dread came over Matt; he knew it was just a matter of time now, and the danger would be real. The Castro guy would find out and come after him. That was why he was in Taos, to locate the rifles—or whoever had them. Pablo must have given him the green light to take them, sell them for the cash. Matt had a lot to worry about.

At the supermarket door, he walked in, heading for the liquor counter, when Arnold stepped up next to him.

"Going to drown your troubles?" Arnold asked, looking at Matt with bloodshot eyes. His eyes, wrinkled sports coat, and baggy pants, made him look like a musician who had played an all-night session.

"You got that right," Matt said, smiling, surprised to meet him, but glad for his company.

"Hey, my kid likes the typewriter," Arnold said while he was fumbling for his wallet. "He don't know how to type—he just pecks at it. But he wants to take typing in school. He pecks away for hours."

Matt could see Arnold was pleased his son was interested in the typewriter, so for now, put off asking to buy back the machine.

When the lady store clerk stepped up on the opposite side of the counter, Arnold said, "Give me a fifth of vodka—Smirnoff."

Matt, fumbling for money in his shirt pocket, said, "I'll have the same—Smirnoff."

"Like minds, think alike," Arnold said paying the lady clerk. "Hey, where you going to drink?"

"Where I shit, shower and shave, where else."

"Forget that dumpy apartment," Arnold said lifting the vodka bottle in a brown bag, after taking his change off the counter. "Come over to the frame shop—the kid plays basketball after school. He won't be home until dinner time."

"Okay—but I should get some eggs," Matt said. "I cook them hard boiled for the bar." Picking up his vodka in a bag, slow, he added, "Oh-h no I don't—the bar job is over."

"What you mean, Matt?"

"Looks like Alex found somebody who's going to buy the cantina," he said. "And I'm out of my swamper job."

"No kidding," Arnold said, as they walked to the automatic doors on the way out of the supermarket. "When did all this happen?"

"This morning," Matt said as they crossed the street that ran beside the supermarket. "The owner of the ski-lodge came in the bar, and said he was interested. They've been talking all morning."

"Wow, that's a shock," Arnold said as they turned onto the street for the frame shop. "But I got a bombshell too—I hear Karen's going to leave Kozlo—when they get to California."

"How come?" Matt asked grinning, looking at Arnold's house ahead.

"She wants to get married," Arnold said leading the way up the steps to the porch of his house. After unlocking the door, he turned and added, "Kozlo thinks she just wants to get hitched—so she can divorce him—and clean him out—moneywise."

"You never know," Matt said grinning, following Arnold through the cluttered workshop, to the kitchen out back. "Hey, where'd you hear all this?"

"My lady friend has a daughter at school with Marci's Elizabeth, and Elizabeth heard Karen tell her mother—her plans—when she gets to California. It was just before she left with Kozlo."

"'It's true that bad news travels fast," Matt said while sitting down at the kitchen table. "The speed of light."

"Elizabeth told my lady friend's daughter, when Elizabeth came over to ask if my lady friend's daughter could come with her and the baby to the hospital—with Marci. They both are skipping school today—to take care of the baby. I was there, I heard."

Smiling, Matt said, "I wonder if Elliott has any idea of what he's getting into over there at Marci's house—with that bunch of women."

"Elizabeth took Marci's being injured—pretty hard," Arnold said lifting a large bottle out of the refrigerator. "We only got Squirt for a mix—my kid polished off all the orange juice—the morning."

"Squirt's okay," Matt said watching Arnold pour the soft drink into the glasses he had half-filled with vodka, then sit down at the table, and slide a glass across.

"Here's to the old days at the cantina," Arnold said lifting his glass.

"Here's to being un-employed—again," Matt said before taking a drink.

"Maybe—the new owner will keep you on, Matt."

"Nah, it won't be the same—anyhow."

"Yeah," Arnold said looking in his vodka glass, "seems the whole thing here—is breaking up—the old crowd—scattering."

"Looks like it," Matt said, feeling his concern about the rifles pressing on him again. He wondered, if he told Arnold about the rifles, what he would say.

"Monk came in the bar to shoot pool," Matt said instead of talking about the rifles, then sipped the last of his vodka.

"You mean Monk came down from his mountain cabin—away from his—bad poetry factory? I wonder what it was that pried him loose?"

"He didn't say," Matt said watching Arnold reaching for the vodka bottle. "He came in with some guy wearing an old army fatigue hat."

"That's Cloyce Maxwell."

"I don't know him," Matt said, watching Arnold pour Squirt on top of the vodka in the glass. "But I think I saw him before—wearing a cowboy hat, driving a truck, pulling a horse trailer. He and Pablo were at the house over in the barrio."

"That's Maxwell," Arnold said sliding Matt the fresh glass of vodka across the table. "He and Pablo are pals. They stole a car or truck, years back; Maxwell got caught, Pablo got away.

The judge let Maxwell join the army—instead of going to jail. He never came back to Taos—permanently. He lives in Texas—maybe El Paso. He never came to live in Taos again."

"That must be the guy then," Matt said, before sipping his vodka.

"But what's he doing here in Taos?" Arnold asked. "Pablo's in the clink down in Santa Fe. Maxwell's dad owned the fence company here in town, but he died two years ago."

"I think I know," Matt said, feeling the heavy wave of fear coming back over him. "I think—it might be the stolen rifles—from the hardware store."

"How come you think that?" Arnold said while leaning back in his chair, still holding his vodka glass on the table.

"I—was trying—to keep it secret," Matt said feeling relieved with talking about it, "but I saw Pablo stash the rifles—after the hardware store robbery—in the well of the barrio—from the back window of my apartment."

"Damn," Arnold said, and with his mouth open, making his face go loose, slack, he added softly, "I figured he had <u>something</u> to do—with that hardware robbery."

"It gets worse."

"What you mean, Matt?"

"I mean I swiped the half-dozen rifles—from the well. I even sold one to Elliott for a hundred seventy-five."

"No shit, man," Arnold said hunching forward, elbows on the table. "You're in deep trouble, Matt. You know that?"

"I know."

"That's why Maxwell is in town—he's come for the rifles. Pablo's headed for jail—Maxwell's going to sell the guns—and maybe split the money with Pablo. When he finds them."

"I hid them good," Matt said, aware now of the danger he was in coming stronger. "I hid them," he said, his throat going dry, choking, "over at Marci's."

"Marci's house," Arnold said in disbelief, shaking his loose, fleshy face from side to side, thinking. "She can get messed up again—even worse, maybe—Elliott too—<u>all</u> of them over there in the Ufer house."

"How you figure that?" Matt asked leaning forward.

"If Maxwell hears the guns are at Marci's," Arnold said in a quiet voice, "and she don't tell him where—she might get hurt, man."

"But she <u>doesn't</u> know," Matt said quickly, "where the guns are."

"That's just it, Matt. When she doesn't talk—she's going to get—clobbered." Arnold leaned back, but still looking at Matt, "Maxwell might even kill her."

"Okay, okay," Matt said, fighting a grin at the exaggeration of Arnold's comment, "then I—just have to move them to a different place."

Arnold looked at the drink in his hand, and said slow, "I'll help—I'll help you."

CHAPTER 22

"Well then," Matt said feeling more guilty about involving Marci now, "we better get over there, move the damn rifles out—while they're all still at the hospital—get Marci off the hook."

When Matt stood up from the table, then drank what vodka was left in his glass, Arnold stood up too, "We'll take my car."

They drove on the highway to the alley in front of Marci's house in Arnold's small K-car, sipping from the vodka bottle Arnold brought along. Arnold turned slowly, hesitating, into the alley.

The rain had started falling steady again.

"No Jeep," Matt said as they neared the driveway next to the house, "they must still be at the hospital."

"Do this quick," Arnold said. "Stuff the guns in the trunk—and jump back in the car."

"That's the furnace room there," Matt said pointing to the door.

Matt pulled open the furnace room door, and feeling in the dark, found the flat box behind the tank. Outside, he closed the door, then leaned to open the car trunk lid, set the box in the trunk quickly, and closed the lid softly.

"Let's get the hell out of here," he said climbing in the car.

"Here man," Arnold said holding out the vodka bottle, as if to prove he could function, drunk or sober.

They were driving up the alley back to the highway.

"Shit," Matt said taking the bottle from Arnold, "look up ahead."

Monk and Cloyce Maxwell were coming across the highway.

"Let me do the talking," Arnold said rolling down the car window.

"Okay," Matt said taking a quick drink from the bottle, at the same time watching the two men ahead.

"Hey, you guys, don't you know it's raining?" Arnold said in a drink-fortified forceful voice.

"You heard that Alex just sold the bar?" Monk said. "He just told us."

"I heard him talking at the bar," Matt said, "but they were just talking—when I left. They hadn't closed the deal."

"Yeah, well it's sold," Monk said. "Alex told us."

"Marci ain't home yet," Arnold said. "We came over to see how she's doing."

"Tomorrow," Monk said, bending to look through the window, across to Matt, "Alex wants us to do an inventory of all the beer and booze in the bar." Then pointing to the vodka bottle, "Let me have a tonk."

When Matt passed the Smirnoff bottle to Arnold, who held it up to Monk, he caught a glimpse of Maxwell leaning over to look at the floor and back seat of the car.

He was checking for the rifles, Matt knew, feeling a coldness running down the back of his neck.

"You guys need a ride?" Arnold asked Monk who was wiping his mouth and beard, while handing the bottle back.

"No, we're just going to the café—on the corner—for tacos," Monk said.

When Arnold held the vodka bottle out to Maxwell, he just shook his head in refusal.

"I thought you were doing laundry," Maxwell said to Matt.

"Guess who I met on the way home," Matt said.

"You want a joint?" Monk asked, to break the confrontation, to keep the conversation friendly.

"Okay," Arnold said. "It's been a while since I had a toke of wacky-tabacki."

Monk gave him a marijuana cigarette with a closed hand through the window, dropping it into his hand.

"You want one, Matt?"

"Nah, I need something—stronger," Matt said meaning whiskey.

"I got some acid," Maxwell said calmly, closing the Marlboro box that he had taken the marijuana cigarette from, and passed to Monk for Arnold.

"I mean—" Matt began.

"Hey," Monk said, "we're getting soaked—we got to run. See you in the morning Matt."

Matt sensed that Monk did not know Maxwell was searching for the missing rifles.

"Maybe, later," Matt said, "We'll hoist a few beers—say good-bye to the bar and Alex—the last day sort of thing."

Monk, hands in his pockets, thought a moment, then bending down to the car window, slowly, "You're right," he said. "Alex has been more to us—than just a bar owner."

"Good idea," Arnold said. "We could even leave a note for Marci—she and Elliott might come over and join us. That would be the whole gang—for the occasion."

Matt smiled; Arnold was really feeling the Smirnoff now, he thought.

"Okay," Matt said to agree with Arnold's enthusiasm, but doubting if Marci would show. "I'll write a note and put it on the door."

"You guys go ahead," Arnold said to Monk. "We'll be over—in a few minutes."

"Okay," Monk said looking for a moment over at Marci's house. "We'll get the pool table—before the evening crowd gets there."

Watching Monk and Maxwell, shoulders hunched against the rain, running back to the highway, Arnold backing up the car, Matt asked, "You got something to write on?"

"There's some cardboard I use for mounting pictures—on the back seat," Arnold said looking in the rear view mirror.

Turning sideways in the car seat, Matt found a piece of cardboard, just as Arnold handed him a ball-point pen from his shirt pocket, before he even asked.

"I wonder if Maxwell believed us," Matt said writing the note. "You think he swallowed that stuff about us coming here to see if she was all right?"

"I don't know," Arnold said stopping the car. "He knows somebody took the rifles—and he's going to stick around until he finds out who."

Matt wondered for a moment, just how Maxwell would go about checking who lived in the apartments at the Romero house.

"What's taking you so long writing that note?" Arnold asked. "You don't have to make it poetry. Just a note, man."

Matt looked at him thinking.

"Maybe it ain't such a good idea—going to the poolroom," he said. "We might slip—and say something that could give the whole thing away."

"Nah, we'll be right under his nose—not hiding, or anything like that," Arnold said and took a sip of vodka from the bottle. "It's not like we're hiding from him; we're acting like we have nothing to hide."

"But he came here to Marci's—he and Monk—<u>caught</u> us here. He might think we were here—to get the rifles from here—if he knows about Pablo—hiding sometimes—in the furnace room."

"Nah—you're thinking too much Matt. Go put the note on the door," Arnold said pointing with the bottle.

"Hey," Matt said, trying to conjure an excuse not to go to the pool room, "what about your kid? Dinner, when he gets home?"

"I made him chili—yesterday," Arnold said holding the vodka bottle with both hands, while looking at Matt. "He loves chili. It's in the fridge—all he's got to do is—warm it up."

Giving Arnold back his pen, Matt held up the note, but could not quench the feeling of foreboding about going to the poolroom, and hesitating, opened the car door, stepping into the rain.

At the door, he ripped a small slot in the cardboard, and hung the note on the doorknob.

"She can't miss that," Matt said when he climbed back into the car, wiping the rain off his face with his hand.

"Maybe Marci won't <u>feel</u> like coming," Arnold said, driving the car slowly toward the highway. "The stitches—and all that."

Matt had the sudden insight, that Elliott could say something about the rifles, a slip of the tongue, if he showed up at the bar with Marci.

"Elliott might blab he bought a rifle from me," Matt said quietly, "if they show up—have a few drinks."

"Elliott ain't that dumb, Matt. But to be sure, <u>tell</u> him to keep quiet about it. Marci too."

Arnold turned abruptly onto the highway, driving away from the Taos Plaza.

"Hey," Matt said, "where you going? The bar's the other way."

"The rifles," Arnold said, "we're going to ditch them—just to be on the safe side. It just came to me, we should hide them."

"I guess you're right," Matt said, grinning, looking at the empty vodka bottle laying on the seat between them. "I didn't think of that. Good man."

At Arnold's house, he drove up the gravel driveway to the rear of the frame house, where the chimney was attached.

"Put the rifles up on the roof," Arnold said quietly, pointing. "Right where it gets flat there, next to the chimney."

"How am I going to reach up?" Matt asked looking through the car window.

"Stand on the car. I'll hand them up."

Matt stood on the slippery roof of the car, rain pelting his face, until Arnold passed up the flat cardboard box. Putting it on the roof, he slid it to the level spot Arnold talked about, next to the chimney.

"Wouldn't the crawlspace under the house—be easier?" Matt asked while climbing off the car top.

"That's the first place they'd look."

"Yeah, I guess you're right," Matt said as they both looked around before getting into the car.

"Hey," Matt said grinning, "what'd you do with the joint Maxwell gave you?"

"I'm saving it," Arnold said as they drove back to town, "for when I have a hangover."

They passed the café at the edge of town on the highway. Matt had never been in there. It was a place most of the local people went, not for the authentic Mexican food, but to meet and gossip in Spanish. Maxwell and Monk were headed there.

As they passed, Matt looked inside the window of the building, completely covered with aqua marine paint, inside and out. A few men in work clothes were sitting on the stools of the lunch counter, was all he could see through the dusty front window.

It crossed Matt's mind, the café would be a good place to hear any gossip going around town. That's why Maxwell was headed there; it sure was not for tacos. He was looking for rifles.

At the bar, walking inside, Matt saw Monk behind the bar that was filled with customers.

"Good crowd," he said to Monk while walking back to the poolroom.

"A tour bus broke down," Monk said. "It's over at the hotel—the brake fluid leaked out. They're sending another bus up from Santa Fe."

"I ain't complaining," Alex said, grinning, as he walked up. "Bring out two more cases of Budweiser, and put them in the cooler. Okay?" he said to Matt, pushing up his eyeglasses higher on his nose.

"Okay, boss," Matt said grinning, and while walking back to the storeroom, heard Arnold order a vodka and orange juice from Monk.

From the hallway, Matt saw Maxwell at the pool table with two guys that he had never seen before. He watched them shooting with cue sticks, all the loose balls, waiting for Monk to come back and start a game.

Maxwell was asking questions, Matt knew, looking for a tip about who might have the rifles. Today, Matt thought, I have to be careful in the extreme. He swallowed, trying to clear the dryness in his throat, before he stepped into the poolroom to get two cases of beer.

As Matt was stacking bottles in the cooler at the bar, he looked up, and saw Marci coming in the door.

She was not wearing the arm sling, only a bandage on her hand. In her good hand, she carried the baby in a basket. Her face looked fresh, her hair in a ponytail swept back, with no make-up.

"How's the hand, Marci?" Matt said when she came up to the bar, standing behind an open stool at the crowded bar.

"No infection," she said softly in a deep rolling voice, setting the basket on the stool, "and it's healing good the doctor says. He wants me to do physical therapy stuff—later."

"Where's Elliott?" Matt asked looking at the door.

"He took the Jeep to the garage," she said before turning to look at the open table at the back of the room. "The fuel pump, or the carburetor is leaking gas." Picking up the baby basket, she said before she stepped back, "Hey bring me a rum and coke—at the table."

Back at the table she set the basket on the chair near the wall, then sat down.

"Is Elliott coming over?" Matt asked when setting the tall glass drink in front of her on the table.

"Uh-huh," she said moving the swizzle stick, stirring the drink, "as soon as he gets done at the garage."

She said it, knowing Matt was thinking about getting her alone.

"What you think about Alex selling the cantina?" Matt asked, sitting down in the chair across from her, grinning, as if saying he was available.

"It doesn't surprise me none," Marci said lighting a cigarette with a paper match. "Doris never liked the bar—and Taos—even less. She told me—one night when we were sitting at the bar. She said she likes being in a city," Marci said while checking the baby for a moment, pushing down the blanket around its face. "Doris probably talked Alex into selling the place on the drive up north to the funeral."

Matt grinned. "She had a lot of time to work on him—going up north." Then Matt leaned forward on the table, saying, "When are you and Elliott going to—?"

"Shit," Marci said blowing a gust of cigarette smoke to one side, "now his wife wants part of Elliott's commission money for the luxury house, the client is building here in Taos—she claims she's entitled to part of the dough Elliott's getting for the design fee."

Marci began chewing on the paper match pack; Matt watching her, wondered if Elliott told her about buying the rifle. Her consternation over Elliott's wife, going over his head.

"She claims that luxury house was begun when they were still married and living together—when the client gave the okay to the design plans."

Matt leaned back in the low bar chair saying, "Aw-w—he'll get more—commissions. Big money is moving into Taos. Even that Hopper guy is thinking of moving here."

"But Elliott's damn near broke," Marci said lifting her drink, the deep tone of her voice coming strong. "With child support for his two youngest kids—he might have to file for bankruptcy."

"Yeah," Matt said, "but he's a professional—and architects have the potential—to make big money. All it takes is the right contract—for some big project, and the money rolls in."

"But that's not today," Marci said, setting her drink on the table. "If you would have moved in my place, honey, at least I'd know what's going to happen tomorrow."

"Nah, babe, we'd be like Karen and Kozlo—if I moved in."

"Just the reverse—economically," she said.

"I heard that's up in smoke too," Matt said quietly.

"You heard they're going to split-up, huh?"

Matt nodded, watching Marci take another drink from her glass. He smiled at her.

"Why don't you come over to the house, sometime," she said in her rolling voice in almost a whisper. "Come at noon—Elliott goes to that client's house he's building about then. He's usually gone till about four in the afternoon. We'll have—a drink."

Matt nodded.

"But if I hear that furnace room door creak open, I'm leaving—through the window," he said quietly to her.

"Hey," she said leaning forward, speaking low, "I don't want to sound crazy—but I've heard that door—creaking again. I'm sure of it—the other night."

"But Pablo is in the clink down in Santa Fe."

Behind Matt, Maxwell came out the poolroom, followed by the two local guys, who looked long-faced. They must have lost big, Matt thought.

Then, Maxwell paid for his beer, standing at the bar next to Arnold, flashing a twenty-dollar bill, and Matt knew for sure the locals got cleaned out.

"Nothing like easy money," Matt said to Marci, who was watching also.

"Wish you had money," Marci said putting her good hand on the baby basket. "If you'd give up that damn scribbling," she said softly, "and get steady money—we'd be able to screw the days away—like we want to."

"You'd have me doing the same stuff Maxwell does—and that crazy Pablo—if—I had the guts to do it," Matt said. "But it wouldn't work—pushing dope is not for me—I just have to keep scribbling."

"I didn't exactly mean drugs, honey," Marci said, "you know that. You're deliberately exaggerating," she said. "I was talking a real job."

She began tearing the matchbook cover off, while adding, "Be careful around that Maxwell," speaking in a whisper. "Sometimes he gets wild—does crazy things."

She put the sulphur striking part of the matchbook in her mouth.

"You want to play pool?" Maxwell asked standing over Matt while tipping up his bottle of beer to drink. "I got the table open."

When Matt stood up from the table, Arnold, who stood behind Maxwell, said in slurred speech, "Ah-h, pool—it's just like screwing—either you're good at it—or you ain't."

"Hey," Matt said to him, take it easy with the language." Then looking at Monk working behind the bar, he said, "We only got three—Monk's working the bar for Alex."

"Get Monk from behind the bar," Maxwell said. "We need a fourth player—he'll play if you ask."

Matt saw it as a way to get out of shooting pool, but before he could say anything about skipping playing, he saw Elliott coming in the bar front door.

CHAPTER 23

"Hear you're going to have a new boss," Elliott said to Matt, and despite everyone standing, except Marci, he sat down on one of the low chairs at the table.

Matt saw bags under Elliott's eyes, and he wore a two-day growth of beard.

Before Matt could say anything, Marci asked Elliott, "You get the Jeep fixed?"

"I can pick it up from the garage, tomorrow, they told me," he said to her, while running his hand over his eyes. "I need a scotch and water."

"You better slow down," Marci said like a school teacher, "this morning, you killed almost a whole bottle of Black and White scotch."

Before Elliott could say anything, Maxwell asked from behind him, standing, "You want to shoot pool? We need a fourth guy."

"Yeah, okay," Elliott said. Then, looking at Marci, "Are you going to stay for a while?"

"Just until I finish this drink," she said rocking the baby basket slowly. Go shoot pool. I have to go grocery shopping."

She took the wad of sulphur paper from her mouth and set it in the ashtray, and picked up her rum and coke.

"Here," Elliott said reaching back for his wallet, then taking out at twenty dollar bill, "get me a pint of scotch."

Folding the money, after setting the glass down, taking the bill in her good hand, she looked at Elliott for a moment, then nodded slowly, but did not speak.

Matt saw she was angry about Elliott's drinking.

Maxwell walked to the poolroom, just as the local cowboy and his wife came in, and were climbing on the stools at the end of the bar. This was the cowboy who refused a donation to the cancer fund.

Matt, following Maxwell, heard the cowboy ask Alex what he was going to do, now that the bar was sold. Alex smiled, saying he was thinking of opening a restaurant, or dog grooming shop.

In the poolroom, Arnold ran all the balls in rotation, with swift, hard shots, despite all he had to drink.

"That's pretty good," Elliott said, sitting on a low chair, the top of the pool table at his eye level.

"You can always," Arnold said, waving the pool cue like a music conductor's baton, "tell a good musician—by the way he shoots pool."

On the next shot, he missed sinking the eight ball, and it bounced off the side bank and rolled out to the center of the table.

Everybody laughed.

"Yeah, Arnold," Elliott said, "you sure got that right."

Smiling, Maxwell began taking the balls out of the table pockets, setting them in the triangular rack in the center of the table. He and Elliott would play against Matt and Arnold.

Elliott was to break the cluster of balls, in the triangle formation, when the rack was removed, and he stood up, finished the scotch in his glass, setting the glass on one of the stacked empty beer cases.

"I bought some ammunition today," he said in a matter-of-fact tone. "Tomorrow—I'm going to sight-in my new rifle," he added, in an almost distracted voice to Matt, who flinched.

Everyone in the room acted as if they did not hear; treating what Elliott said, as if it was just a passing thought on his mind, he wanted to get off.

Matt looked at Maxwell, studying him for a reaction but saw none.

When Elliott shot the white ball, scattering the clustered balls around the table, then began shooting the balls into the pockets according to their number, Matt saw Maxwell pull his Castro cap down over his eyes, and walk out of the room.

Matt could feel the damage Elliott's rifle comment had made—it was the lead Maxwell was looking for—and it came on a heavy wave that was pressing Matt to the floor. He was afraid now. He did not know what to do.

With a feeling of danger gripping the center of his chest, he broke the cluster of pool balls, and sunk five of the balls in the pockets. He missed the sixth shot, and when he straightened up from leaning over the table, he saw Maxwell, coming back through the doorway, carrying four bottles of beer in a bunch.

"Have a beer," Maxwell said to Matt, holding up the bottles in his hands. "I bought a round."

Taking one of the bottles, the one Maxwell held out to him with his fingers, from the others in the bunch, Matt wondered why Maxwell was being so generous, all of a sudden. It was not like him; but Matt took the beer, feeling uneasy about it.

"You must feel lucky," Elliott said, taking one of the bottles. "Or you're sure we're going to win this game."

Everybody had put ten dollars in the pot; the two winners take all.

"I need a break from vodka," Arnold said, and took the bottle handed him.

"Alex told me," Matt said, trying to show calm, "the new boss of the bar wants me to stick around—work for him."

He was talking to Elliott next to him, who was reaching to take the bottle Maxwell was holding out to him.

"You didn't say no, huh," Elliot said, before drinking from the beer bottle. He was standing next to Matt, holding his pool cue, totally unaware of what his rifle comment started.

"Maybe I'll get a raise," Matt said, looking at the beer bottle in his hand before taking a drink. Foam was rising out of the opening, running down the neck. "Hey," he said, "my beer is bubbling."

"Must have been shook up—from me walking," Maxwell said and took a long drink from his bottle.

"It's not warm," Matt said and took a long drink from the bottle. He did not want to be critical, but his suspicion was still there, and he did not know why.

"The glass feels cold—I don't see—how—" he said, but was interrupted.

THE CARROT, THE STRING, AND THE STICK

"Gangway," Elliott said. "My turn to shoot."

He set his bottle on the edge of the pool table, and bent low over the green surface to line up his shot.

Matt clutched the edge of the table suddenly, dropping his bottle to the floor, "Whoa-a," he said holding his mouth open with astonishment, "the table is moving."

Elliott stood up straight, startled, looking at him.

"Shit," Matt said, "the floor is full of spaghetti—I'm standing in blue spaghetti—up to my knees."

"You better sit down, Matt," Arnold said taking hold of his arm. "Over here, man."

"What's happening to me?" Matt said when he sat down on the beer cases. "I'm dizzy—the whole room is bending."

"You're on something," Arnold said. "It sounds like you're hallucinating, kid."

"What was in—that beer?" Matt said leaning to one side. "Wha-at was in that—fucking beer—Maxwell?"

"Hey, Matt," Arnold said quietly, "take it easy."

"Maybe it's LSD," Elliott said. "People talk like that—when they take acid—you got to hold on, Matt, you got to control—"

Maxwell stepped in front of Matt and said, "People who accuse other people—they wind up in a ditch—laying in a ditch."

"Big deal," Matt said. "It started—after I drank the beer you gave me—I started seeing all this crazy shit—these colors. What you expect—me to say?"

"I bought everybody a beer," Maxwell said, holding the pool cue across his chest, the way a rifle is held. "And you're cussing me out now—talking I dropped some drug on you—you who's half-drunk—most of the time."

"Maybe," Arnold said, "we should break this game up—play some other night. What you say—everybody?"

"What you say?" Maxwell asked Elliott. "You want to break-up the game?"

Elliott knew Maxwell was Marci's source for marijuana, now that Pablo was gone, and he did not want to cross Maxwell. He did not want to mess up her source, so diplomatically, he said, "Matt can't play anymore. The game's already over."

"You guys can play," Arnold said putting his cue into the wall rack. "C'mon Matt, I'll give you a ride home."

"My head feels like there's a buzz-saw running inside," Matt said sliding off the stack of beer cases, getting on his feet, dropping his pool cue on the table. "My brain is going a thousand miles an hour—I'm flying—and I can see—everything."

"Hey," Arnold said taking hold of his arm, "you better go home—sleep it off."

"Yeah," Maxwell said, "go home to Romero's—and sleep it off—and we'll talk later. I know where to find you—"

Matt stepped toward Maxwell, "You bastard—you belong in jail—with your asshole pal—Pablo."

Maxwell lifted his left arm, and took a shiny switchblade knife out of his sleeve. When he pressed the button the long blade flicked open, and he held it up like a sword.

"What role you playing now?" Maxwell said. "You trying to play tough guy?"

Arnold pushed Matt from the back toward the doorway before he could speak or make any move.

Matt stumbled, almost falling to the floor. When he stood upright on his feet, Arnold pushed him again, through the doorway, out into the barroom.

"That son of a—" Matt said, trying to turn around, when Arnold pulled him by the arm.

"Let's go, kid," he said, "you've had enough trouble for one night."

"He can't get away with that crap," Matt said in a loud voice.

Alex, talking at the bar with the man named Dents, whose young wife was in the mental institution, overheard what Matt said.

"What crap?" Alex asked Arnold. "Is there trouble back in the poolroom?"

"We all had too much to drink, that's all," Arnold said to Alex, waving his hand to appear casual. "You know how it goes? When money is involved—everybody is right."

Matt was pulled by Arnold toward the door, while he was asking Dent, "How's your wife—doing—in the hos—?"

"Her folks came down from Calgary," Dent said over the talking of the bar customers. "They took her home."

"Good," Matt said before being pulled out the door into the cold night air. "Everybody—should go—home, right Arnold?"

"C'mon, man," Arnold said, "let's get to the car—while the getting is good." When he looked back, while leading Matt down the alleyway to the car, no one came out of the bar.

Riding in the car, Matt said, while holding his head, "I'm going to get one of those rifles—and go back—and fix that bastard Maxwell."

"Don't talk crazy, man," Arnold said, "then you'd be in trouble with the law." He turned on the street where the frame shop was located.

"Hey," Matt said looking up the street, "this ain't the way to my apartment."

"Use your head, Matt. Maxwell's on to you about the rifles. You know he's going to come after you. You got to stay away from there," he said, putting on the car breaks, his shop ahead, off to the left.

"Big deal," Matt said.

Turning into the driveway of the house, Arnold said in a calm voice, "You want some advice?"

"What kind?"

"You better run," Arnold said turning off the car lights, opening the door. "Leave Taos, kid. It's the only way—to get away from Maxwell—and be safe."

"You mean go home—because of Maxwell?"

"Yeah," Arnold said as he stepped out of the car. Looking back at Matt, who sat rubbing his eyes under the overhead dome light, he added, "he's thinking of cutting you up—get those rifles."

"I feel terrible," Matt said. "My mind is swimming."

"What else can you do, Matt? It's too dangerous to stay here in Taos."

"I've got a wad of money," Matt said. "I guess I'd better catch a train—to Detroit. Like a little kid, I'm going to run home and hide under the bed," he said waving his hand, still sitting in the car.

"Can you drive me down to Santa Fe? That's where you get the train. I'll give you twenty bucks."

"I can't leave my kid home—by himself," Arnold said, in a tone that suggested he would drive to Santa Fe. He closed the car door and the dome light went out.

"Take him along," Matt shouted, sitting in the dark car.

"I guess that might work," Arnold said pulling open the car door. "I can buy some supplies for the shop down in Santa Fe—even write the trip off as a business expense."

When Arnold came back to the car after going in the house, the kid followed him out, carrying a pillow and a Mexican striped blanket.

Matt watched him climb into the back seat of the car.

"How come you got to go home," the kid said before he slammed the car door, "in such a hurry?"

"Ah-h," Matt said, "I got a telegram my mom is real sick." Then looking over at Arnold climbing in the driver's seat, said, "Hey, you brought the other bottle of vodka."

"It's for me, not you," Arnold said.

"Right," Matt said, closing his eyes for a moment. "And neither do you—need it.

But you just reminded me—I left my book manuscript—in my apartment. I can't go—without it—it's five month's work. I got to go get it."

"You can't go to your apartment," Arnold said starting the car motor, "and you—know better than me—why."

"Okay, then," Matt said, "you go in and get it—it's on the table in a big manila envelope. You can't miss it."

Arnold was silent for a moment, then after backing down the driveway, turned in the direction of the Romero apartments.

"Thanks," Matt said, rubbing his forehead slowly.

"You're a pain where a pill can't reach," Arnold said, before he stopped the car at the archway in the wall outside the Romero compound, and ran it.

Coming back out, he handed Matt the envelope and apartment door key, after getting in the car.

"You writers—have a dangerous profession—you know that?" Arnold said, driving up the road toward the highway.

"Sometimes," Matt said quietly, "it looks like that."

He almost said hew as sorry he sold his typewriter, but decided not to upset Arnold more.

When they were driving south on the highway, passing the closed drive-in, Matt took out his wallet, and handed Arnold a twenty-dollar bill.

Arnold set the vodka bottle down on the seat, and took the money, and after a quick look back at the kid, slipped the bill in his shirt pocket.

When he picked up the bottle again, to take a sip of vodka, like he was doing before Matt interrupted him, he said, "Maybe the kid can make a living with the typewriter; he likes to do typing. Maybe he can type stuff for people."

"Tell him not to be a writer," Matt said thinking Arnold must have read his mind about being sorry for selling it, wanting to buy it back. "Writing stores—is dangerous."

Arnold turned to look at the kid.

"He's out like a light back there," Arnold said. "I wish I could buy him a gas station—or something—so he could make a living after I'm gone. I'm worried—about how he's going to get along—when I ain't around any more."

"What about the frame shop?" Matt asked, trying to appear concerned.

"He don't show no interest in the work," Arnold said then sipping vodka. "That's what worries me—he's slow—he don't learn fast. At school—the kids poke fun at him."

"The frame shop has to deal with customer who are artists," Matt said. "He won't be missing anything—dealing with artists—who are mostly crack-pots."

"Yeah," Arnold said, "you can say that again." Then after a sip of vodka, he asked, "Hey, what about all your clothes and stuff—at Romero's?"

"When I get home, I'll write a letter to Romero," Matt said quietly, putting his hand on his forehead. "I'll ask him to pack all my things in my duffle bag and send it. I'll send him some money for the cost."

"Hell of a thing," Arnold said, "the way things are working for everybody—we know around Taos."

"Yeah," Matt said, "that's because everybody's chasing his own carrot out here—a carrot on a string."

"What the hell you talking about, Matt?"

"I'm not sure," Matt said quietly, "but my brain is riding a roller coaster—I'm flying downhill."

"Good thing," Arnold said looking at him for a moment, "you didn't drink that whole bottle of beer—you wouldn't have a mind."

CHAPTER 24

Arnold nudged Matt who had fallen asleep, and was dreaming, making noises.
"You, okay?"

"Yeah," Matt said wiping his eyes with his hand. "I was dreaming about Detroit—and I was standing in line to vote."

"Vote? That is—weird, man," Arnold said grinning, lifting the vodka bottle for a sip. "Voting."

"I was in this school hallway," Matt said rubbing the side of his face, "I could see it real clear, and standing behind me was a fat neighbor lady. She lived on my street, three houses away from ours, with her husband Otto. They had worked for some wealthy family in Grosse Pointe until they retired. She was a cook, and Otto was a chauffeur. They had no kids—and they were spotless clean—their house—inside and out. And they were quiet—especially during the war—because they were Germans."

"That's what you were dreaming?" Arnold said while putting the bottle down on the seat.

"Yeah, I had just come back home from Canada, and I was living at home to work and save some money. This fat lady says, 'You should not keep coming back home, they way you do.'

We had been talking, then she ups and says that to me—out of the blue."

"It ain't none of her business," Arnold said.

"Yeah, that's what I thought too, but I just smiled."

"What the hell made you think of that, Matt?"

"I don't know," Matt said while rubbing the back of his neck. "My head feels like it's swelling up—it feels like a pumpkin on my neck."

"How's my kid doing back there? Matt, see if he's all right—he's been awfully quiet back there."

Matt turned and looked in the back seat. "He's still sleeping like a log," he said.

"The kids at school gave him a bad time today, so I told him I'd buy him pizza—if he rode with us."

"He must really like pizza," Matt said turning back to look forward. "I wonder—if pizza could help me. Hey, what's all the lights up ahead?"

"That's Santa Fe, man. We're coming into town," Arnold said reaching for the bottle on the seat.

Stopping at a gas station, and while Arnold was pumping gas into the tank, Matt climbed out of the car, looking up at the overhead lights.

"Look at those blue lights," Matt said, "they're so beautiful—"

Racking the gas nozzle in the holder, Arnold said, "Yeah, they're fantastic. I'm going to ask inside where we get the train."

When he came out of the station store, he said to Matt, still looking up, "We got to go to a town named Lamy—the damn train don't come here to Santa Fe. We got to go ten miles or so—further south."

"Those lights," Matt said. "I want to drink—those lights. I want—to get inside that blue."

"Quiet down," Arnold said opening the car door on the driver side. "You'll wake up the kid."

"Da-ad," came a small voice from the back seat. "I'm getting hungry."

Turning in the front seat, Arnold held out a dollar, "Get some peanuts—or something—to hold you. We got to go a little further—and when we come back here—we'll get a pizza."

"Kids used to pick on me too," Matt said while they were sitting in the car waiting. "I started high school when I was thirteen—and in the swimming pool, I had a small dink—and they made jokes about me."

"Life is hard on people," Arnold said looking at the gas station door for the kid, "who are different—not one of the regular crowd."

"Yeah," Matt said looking in the station store direction, "that's why I liked Marci—she didn't care if you were a freak or not. All people in an art colony should be like her."

"She's one of a kind," Arnold said watching the kid coming across the driveway, carrying a large bag of potato chips.

"If you fill up on chips," Arnold said as the kid climbed into the car, "you won't have room for pizza."

"I won't eat the whole bag," the kid said.

"Okay," Arnold said starting the car.

"We had a neighbor at home," Matt said as they were driving out of the gas station, "and he didn't like me being around—because he had two daughters."

Arnold lifted the vodka bottle and took a sip, listening.

"You know what he did?" Matt said quietly. "To get even he put in a replacement driveway—two cars wide—and had the cement workers slant it toward my dad's yard. When it rained, the run-off flooded my dad's yard—we had a regular frog-pond in back."

"The world is full of people like that," Arnold said, reaching in back over the seat.

"Give me a handful of chips," he said to the kid. "They smell good."

There was the sound of the bag crunching, and Arnold brought out a cluster of chips in his fingers. He drove with one hand, eating chips with the other.

"I had some neighbor trouble like that in California," he said eating. "A neighbor told my wife he didn't like me practicing clarinet half the night. And later, I think he did something to the sewer pipes out front of our house—made the water back up into our basement.

There was no sense going to court—he was some kind of city inspector—the judge wouldn't be fair."

As they drove up to the Lamy road sign, Matt asked, "What does that name mean in Spanish—I never heard of it?"

"I think it's the name of a bishop, or cardinal," Arnold said. "There's a big church here—and a lot of people come here—but I don't know why."

"Well," Matt said, "as long as the train stops here." Then pointing, he said, "Over there is the ticket office."

After Matt bought a train ticket, and was walking back to the car, Arnold climbed out, closing the car door easy, "The kid's sleeping again."

"My head feels like a jet engine is running inside," Matt said quietly. "I can't turn it off. Maybe if I get some sleep—on the train—"

"It's probably LSD," Arnold said lighting a cigarette. "It'll ware off in time—you might get flashbacks for a while."

"I'd like to shoot that Maxwell bastard," Matt said lighting a cigarette. "Doping my beer—like that."

"Yeah," Arnold said dropping his cigarette, "then they'd put you in jail—"

"Maybe," Matt said looking at the large church across the rail tracks, "I'll take a trip to Europe—see Spain—Italy. Do some writing over there for a while."

The train was coming, the lights out front, lighting the track.

"Hey," Matt said, "what you going to say if Maxwell asks—if I told you about the rifles?"

"I thought about that," Arnold said slowly stepping on his cigarette, burning on the ground, "and I'm going to say you needed money so bad, you sold me your typewriter. You were crazy. I'll say that I paid you with drinks—but we never talked rifles."

"I hope it works," Matt said. "And I hope you don't get the LSD treatment." Turning to look at the train, he said, "Well, Chicago here I come."

"I don't have enough money to buy a rifle—Maxwell knows that," Arnold said, watching the train slowing down at the rail platform.

"That line might work," Matt said.

"Well," Arnold said, "I guess it's time for me to say good luck—with your writing—or whatever you're going to do—back east."

"I'll need a lot of good luck," Matt said. "I'm like that donkey—I keep following that carrot dangling on a string—in front of my nose."

"You never know." Arnold said, "What's coming next, up the road." He was shouting over the hiss and clanking of the stopping train. "Besides, living in a quiet suburb—it wouldn't work for you—you'd go nuts."

After shaking hands, Matt climbed up the steps of the train, and over his shoulder, saw the Peter Lorre guy come out of the ticket office. He was carrying a suitcase, and wearing the same tan raincoat.

"Son of a bitch," Matt said. "He's following me."

"Wha-at?" Arnold shouted.

"Seagulls," Matt said in a loud voice. "I keep hearing seagulls."

"This is New Mexico," Arnold shouted. "There ain't no seagulls in a desert."

Nodding, Matt said, "Don't bet on it," and turned to enter the doorway of the train car.

Inside, he took a window seat in the nearly empty coach.

He was exhausted, and with his head resting against the dark glass, he fell asleep even before the train began to roll.

His mind was still racing, the silly phrase from a movie, "Sweety-chickie-baby-pussycat," running through his mind.

Along with the silly phrase, was one of the general orders for a soldier on guard duty; "Pass on all calls to the sergeant of the guard." It was the only one of the elven he could remember in the army.

Matt woke up, when his face slid down, suddenly, on the cold glass window.

He sat up, rubbing his eyes with his fingers, when he heard, "Sweetie-chickie-baby-pussycat," from behind in a thin voice.

Matt turned around and saw a young boy, four or five, standing, holding the back of his seat, his mother next him, smiling.

"Sweetie-chickie-baby-pussycat," the child repeated, looking at Matt.

Thinking a moment, Matt turned back to sit forward, in shock. He thought the words were passing in his mind, being recalled. He was unaware, that he was <u>speaking</u> while he slept.

"You talk in your sleep," the Peter Lorre guy said from across the aisle, lowering the magazine he was holding.

"And I've seen you around Taos," Matt said, "are the words I'm speaking now."

"Yes, yes," the look-alike Peter Lorre said, smiling, "I'm travelling from California—across country to Montreal. And I've taken—side trips—to Santa Fe—and Taos."

Matt saw Peter Lorre had removed his shoes, and was wearing corduroy slippers, the mark of a seasoned traveller.

Suddenly Matt realized where he had seen that face. He sat staring for a moment: LIFE magazine. This guy was in a photograph, showing two other guys, sitting on the bench seat in a DC-3 airplane with him. They all held papers in their hands, and all wore tan raincoats. They were all CIA employees flying to Korea from Japan, when the plane crashed in China.

The article in LIFE magazine, the old magazine copy thrown out at the library in Taos, that Matt had picked up, to look through when he had no money to go to town, reported the men in the photo were prisoners of the Chinese.

Matt rested his head on the back of the seat, when he felt dizzy again, thinking to himself that it cannot be the CIA following him. They would have no reason.

Glancing into the dark corner up ahead in the coach, Matt saw a distorted man lurking in the shadow. He was contorted, one shoulder higher than the other, as if trying to hide his face by twisting. The face had a long nose, and was leering, showing large teeth.

To Matt, the leer seemed to be saying, you have no secrets from us.

Closing his eyes, Matt blocked out the twisted figure. The thought that came to him now, was the question, "What have I got into this time?"

While trying to sleep, the name Bertrand Labec was the Peter Lorre guy's name from the photograph Matt remembered, from the magazine article. He was imprisoned in China.

In Chicago, when Matt was changing trains, getting the Wolverine that crossed southern Michigan to Detroit, he saw the Peter Lorre guy climbing on the coach up ahead.

"Yeah," Matt said to himself, "he crosses to Canada from Detroit—to get the train to Montreal. That figures."

On the Michigan train, watching the farms going by outside Battle Creek, Matt could feel the buzzing was lower inside his head, the <u>clack</u>-<u>clack</u> of the rails, louder than the buzz of LSD.

The train pulled into Detroit at noon, and Matt walked quickly through the terminal looking for the telephone booths.

"Yeah, mom," Matt said talking, while juggling his book manuscript under his arm, "I'm here in Detroit. I'll get a taxi—I should be home in about an hour."

His mother asked, "What—are you going to do now?"

"Get a job," he said, shaking his head about the question, "maybe write for a newspaper. We'll talk about it later."

Matt always felt uneasy talking about getting a job. He could never convince himself he belonged working steady at some writing tasks he did not believe were important.

"You and that writing again, Matthew," his mother said in a disparaging voice. "We've never had—a writer—in our family."

Matt was not sure when he started on the path to write stories, but he remembered how interested he was at two or three years old, when his mother read him tales of elves, princesses and castles.

At grade school, he was not interested in classes, until he read, "The Sire de Maletroit's Door," and "The Gift of the Magi," and something pulled him toward fiction.

Then in high school, the dreary classes fell away, when he discovered in English Literature, stories such as "Rossum's Universal Robots" and "Leiningen and The Ants." He began reading every fiction book he could find.

On television, he found the Somerset Maugham stories dramatized, and watched, devouring the plot lines.

He read in most his spare time, he remembered. Then like everyone who reads prolifically, he tried writing stories, and found himself in conflict with daily reality, by spending most of his time scribbling.

He was not interested in money, and as far as the world was concerned, he was a derelict.

Now talking on the phone, he was trying to explain himself.

"Mom, we'll talk about this later," Matt said, hoisting the manuscript envelope that was slipping under his arm. "I'll explain everything to you and dad when I get home."

"I'll get your room ready, son," his mother said in a tone that dismissed the conflict over writing. "By the time you get here, I'll have the bed made."

"Thanks mom, goodbye."

Stepping out of the phone booth, Matt stopped short.

In front of him, the Peter Lorre man was standing at the side of the phone both, leafing through the pages of the phone book hanging on a chain.

Matt knew he had been listening to his phone conversation.

"So you got off in Detroit?" Matt said calmly.

"Yes, yes," the short man said smiling up. "Over in Windsor, I get the train—to Montreal." He coughed, then said, "I have friends—here in Detroit—I'm looking for their phone number. I want to call them."

Matt noticed he was looking through the yellow pages.

"Well," Matt said holding the book manuscript out toward the door, trying not to show his anger at being followed, "I've got to run—I'm expected someplace."

He turned away abruptly.

In the taxi, Matt noticed a car following, but it stopped at the corner, when the taxi turned onto Matt's home street. Matt watched through the rear taxi window, as the car turned around and drove away.

"Maybe it's got something to do with my last trip to Spain," Matt said to himself.

Then he leaned forward, and pointed out his parent's house for the taxi driver.